UNDER AN EVIL STAR

Jane Holland

Copyright © 2020 Jane Holland

All rights reserved.

Published by Thimblerig Books

ISBN: 9798648619968

The moral right of the author has been asserted.

No part of this book can be reproduced or transferred by any means without the express written permission of the author.

All characters in this story have no existence whatsoever outside the imagination of the author, and have no relation whatsoever to any person or persons coincidentally bearing the same name or being employed in the same profession or living in the same area.

Everything in this story without exception has been conceived in the imagination of the author and no person or event in the story is even remotely inspired by real life.

Other fiction by Jane Holland

GIRL NUMBER ONE (#1 UK Kindle Chart Bestseller)
LOCK THE DOOR
FORGET HER NAME
ALL YOUR SECRETS
LAST BIRD SINGING
MIRANDA (WHY SHE RAN)
THE HIVE
DEAD SIS

UNDER AN EVIL STAR
(Stella Penhaligon Thrillers 1)

THE TENTH HOUSE MURDERS
(Stella Penhaligon Thrillers 2)

THE PART OF DEATH
(Stella Penhaligon Thrillers 3)

PROLOGUE

Jack fumbled for the phone, shocked awake by its shrill ringing next to his bed. It was dark in the bedroom, no light showing through the curtains yet.

What the hell was the time?

'DS Jack Church,' he muttered, slurring his words, still partly in the shadowy world of his dream.

'Jack?' The familiar voice was shaky. Scared, even. 'Oh God, Jack … '

He struggled up on his pillows, fumbling for the light switch. 'Bernie?' It was his older sister, Bernadine. His heart began to race as she began to stammer something incoherent. Something impossible. What the hell? 'Bernie, slow down, you're not making sense.' He glanced at his digital clock. 'It's the middle of the bloody night. Take a deep breath. Now, what on earth's the matter?'

'It's Chloe,' she gasped.

'Chloe?' Abruptly, he was the one who could barely speak, suddenly sick with dread. Somehow, he forced himself to ask, 'What about her?' But his sister only whimpered, as though words had failed her too. 'Bernie, for God's sake, whatever it is, just tell me.'

'Chloe didn't come home tonight,' she whispered after a long pause. 'I'd been sitting up for hours, waiting for her, you see. In case she was drunk, or … or had lost her key.'

'And?'

'The police were just here at the flat. They said …'

His eyes widened, focusing on the far wall, at a large black-and-white photograph, blown-up and professionally framed, of him and his wife on their wedding day.

Chloe was smiling in the photograph, long hair tumbling back over one lace-covered shoulder, head tipped back as she laughed for the camera, extending one graceful hand to display the glint of her wedding ring. He himself looked dazed and ecstatic at the same time, his gaze locked on her beautiful face, oblivious to the photographer …

'Go on.'

'I tried to look after her, Jack. You can't blame me for this. I did my best, I swear it. I know she wasn't happy, but I couldn't be with her twenty-four, seven. And now …'

'Bernie, please.'

'Oh, God.' He heard the strain in her voice, and knew what she would say even before she said it. 'Jack, she's dead.'

'No.' He stared at Chloe in the photograph, speaking to her now, not his sister, almost pleading. 'No.'

'That's why the police came.'

'No, I don't believe it. It's not possible.'

'I'm so sorry,' Bernie whispered again, and he could hear that she was crying. 'So, so sorry.'

Jack tried to focus on what his sister was telling him, to stay calm and professional. But he felt like throwing up instead.

The room shrank to a narrow corridor, him and the phone handset he was clutching, and then the photograph opposite. Chloe's gorgeous face laughing back at him.

This couldn't be happening.

'How?' he demanded at last. 'How, in God's name?'

'She went under a train at Hemel Hempstead, they said. About ten-thirty. One of those late night intercities. The police said … Oh Jack, they've seen CCTV coverage of the platform, and they say it wasn't an accident.' His sister sounded beside herself. 'They're saying Chloe killed herself, Jack.'

'No.'

'All I can say is … I'm sorry.' His sister paused. 'Look, I wish this wasn't true. That they'd made a mistake. But they've got her bag, Jack. Her things. They showed me, so that I could … ' She stopped abruptly, swallowing. 'But they need you to come and … You know. Next of kin. To identify the body. So I gave them your details.'

Jack dropped the handset at last. He covered his face with his hands. 'No, no.' He was howling, rocking, pushing the horror away with every ounce of strength in his body. 'No, no, no.'

He pictured his wife's face as he had last seen her, the sharp look in her eyes, all laughter between them gone, and the howl intensified to a shriek.

Dead?

It couldn't be true. Not his Chloe, not his wife.

She went under a train at Hemel Hempstead.

Why would Chloe do such a terrible thing? It made no sense.

They had been happy.

Past tense.

His fault, all his fault. Too many late nights at work, too many times he'd forgotten some important date or dinner, his work consuming everything, and then the miscarriage. He hadn't been there for her. He hadn't listened to her. He knew it all, because she had told him a thousand times without saying a word.

She went under a train at Hemel Hempstead.

Still, it could be a mistake, a misunderstanding. It had to be, surely? Or some dreadful accident.

Perhaps she'd stumbled on the platform. Or she could have been pushed … Or perhaps … Perhaps …

CHAPTER ONE

'Happy Birthday to you, Happy Birthday to you,' they all chorused dutifully, seated around the dining room table as Claire carried in the home-made cake, four candles burning above lavish pink-and-white icing. 'Happy Birthday, dear Julie. Happy Birthday to you!'

Stella snapped an impromptu photo on her phone of Julie beaming with pleasure – a rare occurrence – and urged her friend, 'Blow out the candles!'

'All four of them,' Nick said under his breath, his stubbly chin propped up on one elbow as he lounged beside Julie, still in the soiled blue uniform he'd been wearing at the nursing home that day.

'One for each decade,' Claire told him in a repressive tone, then placed the cake reverently in front of her partner. 'Happy Birthday, darling.' She bent and kissed Julie on the cheek. 'I made it myself.'

'We can tell.'

Ignoring her irritating cousin, which was often the only way to deal with Nick, Claire said persuasively, 'Go on, Julie. Make sure you blow them out at once. Or it's unlucky.'

'Must I? Really? This is all a bit undignified. I feel like I'm four, not forty.' But Julie blew out all four candles while they clapped and cheered her on, then shook her sleek head at them, as though they were no older than the kids she taught at school. 'There, you annoying lot. Satisfied? Any chance I can have some booze now?'

Stella took one last photo, then put her phone away. 'Of course,' she said, and nodded to Nick. 'White wine in the fridge for the birthday girl.'

'And the birthday girl's other half,' Claire said quickly.

Nick reached into the fridge for the bottle, glancing round at Stella. 'How about you, Stell?'

'Not right now, thanks.' Stella grimaced. 'I have to work.'

Julie shot her a hard look. 'On my birthday?'

'I know, I'm sorry, but I'm massively behind.' Stella had taken a week off to drive along the Dorset coast, a place she'd only known scantily before, and stop for a few days with an old friend of hers, Simon Ross. It had been such a relaxing break, and she and Simon had spent most of their time gossiping like mad about their friends in the astrological community, which was always good for her soul. But then she'd come home to find a pile of work waiting for her, and some of it overdue. 'Maybe later tonight?'

'Where's Mel?' Nick asked, and an awkward silence fell over the room. 'Don't tell me she forgot her own mum's birthday?'

Julie said nothing.

'Melanie couldn't get away from uni,' Claire said quickly, and gulped back some wine. 'Too much study work, I guess. Besides, you know what kids are like at that age. She's probably obsessing over some boy.'

'My daughter didn't even send me a birthday text this year, let alone call me to wish her mother Happy Birthday,' Julie said, her voice suddenly icy. To disguise her hurt, Stella thought, seeing the shuttered look on her face. 'Don't make excuses for her, Claire. She's not a child anymore.'

Nick grimaced at Stella, then produced a party popper from somewhere and let it off over the kitchen table. 'Well, we're here for you, love. Never mind, eh? Shall we play charades?'

She stayed at the impromptu kitchen party for another ten minutes, just to be polite, and then slipped upstairs to her bedroom in the house she shared with them all.

As the door closed on music and laughter from below, Stella was aware of a guilty sense of relief.

Though she loved her fellow house-sharers to bits, it was awkward them being so close every day, rubbing shoulders and always in each other's personal space. But she'd probably be on the streets if it hadn't been for Julie and Claire offering her a room in their house.

After chucking in her teaching job at the school where Julie and Claire still both taught, she'd found it hard to pay the rent on her own flat.

She had quickly realised that freelance astrology – her new chosen career – was never going to make her rich. But it was what she'd always wanted, to become a professional astrologer, and this was her chance to make it work. So she hadn't given up, begging around her friends for a sofa to sleep on until she was back on her feet.

To her delight, Julie had rejected the sofa-surfing idea but offered her a bedroom instead, at what was really a peppercorn rent of a few quid a month at first, along with help with the housework and gardening.

Nick, Claire's cousin, had already been living there when she arrived. He worked as a nurse at one of the local residential care homes, and was a bit of a ladies' man in his spare time. Luckily, his hours were fairly demanding, and included some evening shifts, so he didn't get enough spare time to become a real nuisance. After Nick had asked her out a few times, and been politely declined, he seemed to get the message that she wasn't interested and had since left her alone.

Her bedroom was a cramped boxroom at the back of the house. But it overlooked the garden, and had a lovely view of woods and the sea in the distance. Best of all, there was room for a work desk under the window.

Stella turned on the table lamp and sat down at her desk. Outside, it was already dusk, a peaceful spring evening.

She checked her planetary transits, as she did whenever she opened her electronic ephemeris, frowned briefly at today's chart, and then opened her new client's email. If she got this initial reading spot-on, and the chemistry between them worked, this could become a useful long-term contact.

Carefully, she began to type out Nancy's astrological data into discrete fields on the software form.

Nancy Canning.

Date of birth.

Time of birth, which did seem to be accurate rather than estimated or randomly guessed, as it gave odd minutes rather than being rounded up to the hour or half hour.

Then place of birth, or nearest major town or city at least. The longitude and latitude came up automatically as she typed in the name of the city.

Exeter, Devon, England.

Not too far from where she lived in Cornwall, in fact. Just over an hour's drive. She enjoyed occasional visits to Exeter for shopping and meet-ups with other like-minded souls, being only one county across and a little further west.

A dog barked somewhere among the houses clustered around them in the quiet suburban street, and Stella stood up to close the curtains.

There were church bells ringing too, in the distance. She stayed where she was another moment, listening.

Campanologists practising their bell-ringing at the local church; the bells always rang at about this time on a Thursday evening, for an hour or so.

She thought fleetingly of her father, and those troublesome transits on her chart, but put the thought aside. She had work to do and there was no profit in worrying about a thing before it happened. Especially when it might not happen at all, but take another form entirely.

She selected 'Female' under type of chart, then chose 'Placidus' for the house calculation. Sometimes she found the Koch or Even House systems could give better results. But overall, Placidus was her preferred method of house division.

Finally, she hit Calculate, and sat back, watching with a smile as the chart instantly appeared on the screen. Like magic!

'The wonders of technology,' Stella thought out loud.

Her client's chart looked interesting, she thought, leaning forward again to study it more closely. Though, to be fair, she found everyone's chart interesting.

No, *fascinating*.

Mars on the Midheaven. She raised her eyebrows, typed a quick note in the box beside the chart – 'Prone to disputes and conflicts, perhaps especially in her career?' – and then checked the planetary dignitaries.

Her mobile phone buzzed with a notification.

Stella picked it up and glanced at the screen. Her astrology friends on the WhatsApp group were still all chatting excitedly about the recent Saturn-Pluto conjunction in Capricorn. She'd heard enough about it during the run-up to the event though, and had moved on mentally to new things.

Still nothing from her dad, she thought, frowning as she looked back to her messages, in case she'd somehow missed a notification.

Give me a ring, I need to speak to you urgently.

That had been his last message, received after a missed call from his number. Last Sunday afternoon, four days ago now.

She hadn't heard from her father in several years, a fact confirmed by the date of his previous message which had stated bluntly, *Happy Birthday*.

Like Julie's nineteen-year-old daughter, Mel, her dad was not great at keeping in touch. A vicar, he tended to look on her astrological profession with disapproval. 'Astrology is tantamount to black magic,' he'd told her.

At first, she'd decided to ignore his message and not call. What could be so bloody urgent, after all?

She and Dad had fallen out massively after a memorable Christmas lunch at the vicarage when she had got drunk and announced that she didn't believe in God. Worse, that she had never believed in God. Her father had exploded with fury. He'd ordered Stella to pack her bags, and then had thrown her out on her ear, even though she'd only finished university that summer and had nowhere else to go.

Dad always loved a grand gesture.

He'd thrown her mother out too, when Stella was only seventeen. His reasons were still shrouded in mystery, though mum's banishment had followed an argument over Stella's university choices. Horrified, and feeling partly to blame, Stella had gone down to London on the train with her mum, staying for a few days at her aunt's crowded house in Dagenham. She would have stayed with her mum, if she could. But she'd been sitting A-Levels that year at the local school, and she'd needed his support to get through the first year of university at least.

She glanced through her unanswered texts to him.

Tried ringing but you're not answering. What's so urgent?

Dad, answer your phone!

Your phone says it's turned off. Message me back, would you?

Why wasn't Dad replying?

On a whim, she opened a new window on the astrological software and called up her dad's birth chart, plus transits.

There was nothing too horrific happening with his current transits. A minor square to her father's Sun in Taurus, that was all. Harmless enough, she thought, frowning, except that the square was also activating his natal Sun-Algol conjunction.

Fixed stars, she thought with derision.

Caput Algol was a fixed star at 26 degrees of Taurus, an eclipsing binary in Perseus Constellation, right on top of her father's Sun.

The star had a malefic reputation, associated with danger, violence and hanging, among other unsavoury things. Ptolemy had considered it 'the most evil star in the heavens'.

Such dire ancient warnings had no place in modern astrology, though.

How could they?

Still, she sat a while looking at Caput Algol in her father's chart. The Arabian name could be translated as "Head of the Ghoul" from what she recalled, apparently coming from the same origin word as "alcohol". The star was meant to influence those born under its unfortunate, pulsing light into extremism, brutality and disaster.

Hardly things anyone would associate with a vicar in the Church of England, she thought wryly, and closed the chart.

Nearly an hour later, Julie put her head round the door. 'Claire's opening a bottle of champagne,' she said with a smile. 'Seems a bit over the top, but – '

'You deserve it, birthday girl.'

Julie laughed. 'But would *you* like a glass?'

'Thanks, why not?' Stella pushed aside her notepad and stood up. Deliberately, she left her silent phone behind. These people were her family now. 'I could do with a bit of bubbly, actually.'

CHAPTER TWO

The mobile rang, breaking the silence in the bedroom. It rang insistently, just as it had done on the night his sister had phoned to shatter his world, to say that Chloe was dead.

Jack groaned, eyes closed, still half-asleep.

The old nightmare receded slowly into the darkness. His heart was racing, his mouth dry. It felt as though he had only been asleep for a few hours, and a quick glance at the digital clock display confirmed that suspicion.

Five past four in the morning.

Christ Almighty.

He needed to start going to bed earlier. These late nights were becoming ridiculous. But he found it so hard to fall asleep these days, his bedtime continually receding. No doubt one time he would find it was dawn before he could finally let his weary mind and body relax into sleep.

The phone was still ringing.

Slowly, he rolled over, reached for the mobile, and fumbled it to his ear. 'DS Jack Church,' he muttered.

'Sorry to disturb your beauty sleep, sarge.'

It was the annoyingly cheery voice of his young constable, DC Ronny Myles. Twenty-seven and as stringy as a bean.

He closed his eyes again. 'Ron? What the hell?'

'We need you to come in, sarge. How quickly can you get to Tintagel?'

'Tintagel?'

'The castle.'

'Tell me you're kidding.'

Outside his curtains, there was a pale, gloomy light in the sky. By six, he was usually getting into his running gear, ready for a quick half hour run, followed by an even quicker shower, before heading off to work.

He disliked being woken with a phone call, especially when it meant he would need to forego his morning run. Anyway, nine times out of ten it was not what he would class as a real emergency.

'It's a bit bloody early for a shout. This had better be worth it, Ronny. Because if it's just a domestic – '

'How about a severed head, sarge?'

'A what?'

'A severed head. And nothing else.'

'At Tintagel *Castle*?'

'Wide awake now, mate, aren't you?'

Jack swung his legs out of bed, abruptly alert.

'I'm putting you on speaker phone. You can catch me up while I dress.' He grabbed his trousers off the hanger. 'And I've told you before, Ronny, you watch your tone with me. I'm your sergeant, not your bloody mate.'

CHAPTER THREE

Something woke Stella just before dawn. A noise outside in the garden? Her bed was beneath the window – there really wasn't much choice for bed placement in a room this size – so she was easily able to sit up and twitch back the curtain for a look.

The dark had become thin and milky, more greyish-white than black. The garden looked empty. But as she rubbed a porthole in the misted-up window with her fist and peered out, she saw a low shadow slink across the lawn before melting into the hedge at the back.

Too skinny and quick for the local badger, whom they had called Bill and who occasionally lumbered through their small back garden at night.

A fox?

Her mind flashed back to her father and the fox pelt he kept on the wall in his private study. Not in the austere room where he met parishioners to discuss weddings, funerals and christenings, but in the long room with the sloping ceiling at the top of the house – an attic room, really – where he read and studied old books, and kept an assortment of curios and mementoes in glass cases and cabinets.

He habitually kept that room locked, and the key on a chain at his waist, as though the contents of his study were somehow sacred. To him, no doubt they were. But on the rare occasions when she'd been allowed to set foot in his private study, she'd thought it damp and musty-smelling, and recalled asking about the fox pelt once as a child only to have her head bitten off.

'Mind your own business, brat,' her father had said, and shooed her out of his study, locking the door after her and shouting through the keyhole, 'Go and play. That's all you're good for.'

She'd further incurred his wrath by studying drama and media at university, when he'd wanted her to become an accountant. Then she'd managed to get a job teaching drama at a Cornish school for a few years, which he described as a 'Mickey Mouse' career. But the paperwork and constant Ofsted pressures had driven her half mad, and she'd started studying astrology in the evenings and through holidays, desperate for a different life.

Having already taken a foundation course in astrology while at university, she'd managed to speed through the diploma in only three and a half years, then finally taken the plunge and given in her notice at the school. Since then, Stella had struggled to make ends meet as a professional astrologer. But it had been worth it for the sheer freedom of this job.

Her phone buzzed. Her wake-up call. She set it for an early morning wake-up several days a week, so she could put in a quick run or trip to the local gym before starting the working day.

Give me a ring, I need to speak to you urgently.

Why had he sent that message?

Stella rolled out of bed and got dressed. Not in her running gear, or one of her outlandish 'astrologer' outfits that she wore when meeting a client face-to-face – she'd discovered that most clients seemed to expect her to look like a cross between Mystic Meg and a drug addict – but in black jeans and vest top, with a zip-up hoody over the top to keep her warm.

She grabbed her car keys, phone and purse, and tiptoed down the stairs as quietly as possible. Nick's bedroom door was partly open – he often left early – but she knew Julie and Claire would be making the most of the hour remaining before they needed to get up for work.

I need to speak to you urgently.

It felt ludicrous to be worrying about her old dad, a man she had not seen in years and who had probably never lost so much as a moment's sleep over her own behaviour.

But her restless mind would not be still. Not after looking at the transit triggering the malefic Caput Algol-Sun conjunction in his natal chart. Fantasy, perhaps, to imagine a fixed star could spell anyone's doom.

But there'd been the horary chart she had drawn up late last night, to answer the question, 'Is my dad okay?'

Pluto had been exactly conjunct the Midheaven, the sinister planet of death indicating the outcome of the matter, and making a tight square to the chart ruler, while the Moon in the deadly 8th house had been void-of-course.

A clear indication of a 'No,' answer.

CHAPTER FOUR

Haunting in its gloomy, olde-worlde isolation, Tintagel Castle sat on a rocky peninsula, overlooking the rolling, blue-green Atlantic on three sides. A major tourist attraction in Cornwall, the site was spanned at its highest point between island and mainland by a cantilevered steel footbridge, only recently installed by English Heritage.

Jack knew the place well. Too well, he thought, given his current mood.

The castle had been one of his and Chloe's favourite destinations when they first moved down to Cornwall, both of them happy to be posted a long way from their East London roots and keen to learn about country living.

In those days, tourists had walked across on a lower wooden bridge, though no less picturesque ... or challenging for anyone with a fear of heights.

'Oh my God, too high,' Chloe would gasp every time, gripping the bridge rail, and he would help her across, a supportive arm about her waist.

He and Chloe would roam the windswept island for an hour or two, taking photos of the sea and land, and then retreat out of the wind to the little tourist shop and the café, where they served hot drinks and pasties as well as rock cakes as craggy as the island itself.

It wasn't a castle, per se, but the remains of a fortress-cum-medieval hall, built high above the rocky cliffs on the north Cornish coast. There was not much left from those days: areas of uneven paving stones, some weather-worn archways and walls, most of them knee-high at best, a few stretches twice the height of a man, and a general sense of desolation. The ancient buildings had long since tumbled away, or been raided by local masons for stone and brick, or been grown over by grass and brambles.

Below the remains, the Atlantic tide lapped at a shallow bay, grating pebbles on a seaweed-strewn beach and filling vast cavernous holes below the island with its salt swell.

The word 'castle' had stuck though, and somehow nobody questioned it. It was certainly still a stronghold, the steep approach road now blocked off from ordinary traffic, so that the hundreds of thousands of determined tourists who visited every year either paid for the Land Rover ride to and from the castle heights, or walked it.

Today, the dawn light was cool and milky, a sharp wind from the Atlantic shivering through gaps in the stone walls.

DS Jack Church drove straight down the narrow, winding hill, ignoring the No Entry signs, and pulled up beside the other police cars and vans already assembled near the footbridge at the base of the hill.

Ronny came towards him, trouser legs flapping in the wind. 'Up there, sarge!' He pointed towards the long row of steps that led up to the new bridge.

'You're joking.'

'Sorry, sarge. Bit of a hike, I know. But that's killers for you ... ' Ronny grinned. 'No consideration for the police.'

Jack peered up at the near-vertical incline, remembering how he and Chloe had climbed laboriously to the top one time, single-file, in heavy rain.

No steps or handrail then, as he recalled, only a muddy slope, bordered by scrub on one side above the thin sliver of stream that ran noisily from the town of Tintagel above down to the sea.

She'd been in front of him the whole way, finally turning near the top, her face half-hidden by the hood of her yellow anorak, to laugh at his slow progress. 'Stick-in-the-mud!' she'd called him, then hurried on in search of the castle entrance, always lighter, faster, keener than him to do everything.

What had happened to reduce her to the depths of depression so quickly?

But even as he wondered that, Jack knew the answer, and shoved the terrible thought to the back of his head where it had come from. It had been nearly eighteen months since Chloe died. When was he going to forgive himself and move on? Another year? Another two? Never?

One thing was sure. He couldn't keep going round and round the same guilt-ridden territory in his mind. It would drive him mad.

Maybe it already had.

'Sarge?'

Ronny was still waiting.

'Yeah, I'm coming. And enough with the wisecracks.' Jack glanced over his shoulder at the mud-splattered Renault hatchback coming to a halt behind his, and recognised a local reporter behind the wheel. 'We could do without seeing those sort of police "jokes" in the papers. Funnily enough, they never go down well with the public.'

A stretch of high stone wall loomed above them, hiding level ground behind it, some former medieval or later entry point to the castle. Jack followed Ronny up the steps and found a forensic team already on site, gingerly erecting a shelter of some kind against the ancient wall rather than the usual tent.

'What's this?' he asked, frowning.

'Forensics are doing their best. The site manager has asked us to avoid damaging the wall. Apparently, it's very old. Medieval or older. They're keen for us not to make any more holes in it than there already are.' Ronny shrugged. 'But we need to secure the scene, because the bloody head's on it.'

'I beg your pardon?'

'The severed head, sarge. It's been placed on the medieval wall.' Ronny made a face. 'Well, in one of the gaps. Like a vase on a windowsill. Here, take a peep for yourself.'

Jack nodded to the SOCO struggling with the lean-to shelter in the strong winds, and ducked under the flapping white sheet. Plastic sheeting was down and the wall itself was taped off.

The head had indeed been placed in a gap in the stone wall. It looked perfectly central too, at a glance equidistant from each side, though with ample room to spare above the top of the head; for all the world like a neatly arranged vase on a windowsill, as Ronny had said.

Or a trophy, Jack thought.

The head was facing outwards. Staring over the clifftops towards the grey Atlantic in a mess of congealed blood. Its own, presumably.

The hair was a rough tangle of greyish-white, a few strands lifting in the wind. A man's head, almost certainly. But whose?

'Have we taken a look at the face yet?'

'Not yet,' the SOCO came to join him, Cameron, still clinging grimly to the side of the shelter, though the sound of hammering outside suggested someone was trying to secure the structure in place, pinning it to the ground before it could blow away. 'We didn't want to disturb the scene.'

'I need to see the face.'

Ronny had come in behind him. 'You can lean across the tape if you need to, sarge. Photos have been taken of the back of the head, and the surrounding wall and grassy area. But not the front.'

Hurriedly, Cameron said, 'I'll get the photographer back in if you're going to turn him round. She tried to get to the other side of the wall, but it's a sheer drop out there. Health and safety nightmare.'

'Definitely a man?' Jack asked Ronny, though he was fairly certain of the answer.

'Oh, I'd say so, sarge. Wouldn't you?'

'And no sign of the rest of him?'

'We've searched within about a two to three hundred yard radius of this point, but found nothing. As soon as we get more bodies on site, I'll widen the search to include the cliffs on this side of the castle, and the island itself. It'll probably take a day or two to be certain. But the whole site's been closed to the public now, so that'll speed things up.' Ronny shrugged. 'If there's any more of this poor bastard to be found here, sarge, we'll find it.'

Jack glanced at the SOCO. 'Get the photographer, would you?'

Cameron nodded and came back a moment later with the photographer in tow, a woman in forensic whites, who seemed unmoved by the grisly nature of the scene.

Jack sighed. 'Ronny, gloves.' A pair of gloves was found for him, and carefully, with the others watching, he unglued the head from its sticky blood, lifted it a couple of inches or so – surprisingly heavy, he thought, fighting the urge to throw up – and turned it around.

The photographer set to work at once, her flash going off repeatedly, illuminating the grisly find for them on its sticky shelf.

'Okay,' Jack said, staring into the parchment-coloured face, still with grey, bedraggled beard attached, 'who the hell are you?'

CHAPTER FIVE

Stella had planned to go straight to the vicarage that morning, but a small group of men and women in woollen hats and anoraks by the lychgate caught her attention. She parked beside the remote church, alongside the other cars, and went to find out why they were there. Perhaps there was an event this morning at the church, and her father would be found inside. She did not particularly want a public scene, if he was in one of his difficult moods. But there was no point going to the house if he was in the church.

The Church of St. Joshua and its associated vicarage were situated in the middle of nowhere, about a hundred yards from a crossroads.

Once upon a time, her father had told her, there'd been a thriving country community based out here in the wilds of north Cornwall, where locals would have walked or ridden to church down any one of the four narrow, winding country lanes that intersected there.

These days, although the nearest town was beginning to grow beyond its seaside sprawl, Pethporro's boundary was still several miles from the church. And the number of rural residents had dropped severely over the past century, with the result that few people came to the church for actual services. Though it was occasionally used as a community centre or for ramblers to visit as part of a Cornish church tour.

'Hello,' she said to a woman in a tweed jacket holding a cardboard box. 'Something happening at the church today?'

'There was meant to be a jumble sale at eleven,' the woman told her, 'only the Reverend hasn't opened up for us yet. It's every third Friday of the month, he can't have forgotten. He knows it's nine o'clock sharp for setting out the tables and getting the tea urn on. But there's no sign of him.'

'Have you tried the vicarage?'

'Of course we have.' The middle-aged man beside her, probably her husband, took the box from his wife and gave Stella a scathing look. 'We walked over there first, in case he'd forgotten. But the vicar isn't in, or isn't answering the door. Though all this has been arranged for weeks, and my wife emailed a few days ago, just to confirm. It really isn't right.'

The woman nodded helplessly. 'I should have known something was wrong when the Rev didn't email me back. But I just assumed he was busy.' She bit her lip. 'Now what are we going to do? All these people have turned up, ready to set out the stalls, and we can't get into the church. And what about when the public turn up at eleven?'

Stella frowned, her uneasiness growing. 'And he's not in the church?'

'I don't think so,' the man said. 'All the doors are locked, and we walked all the way round, shouting.'

'Sounds like I should head over to the vicarage myself.' Stella tried to hide her concern. 'Maybe I'll have better luck. He is quite a heavy sleeper.'

One of the other men came closer, peering over the man's shoulder in a puzzled way. 'Sorry, is it Stella? The Rev's daughter?'

It was one of the church wardens, Peter Harbut. Fair-haired and slim, he was a pleasant enough man in his forties, and lived about a mile away in a large house on the outskirts of Pethporro. Peter worked in town as an accountant, she seemed to recall, and had some old family connection with the church. He had been away in London for years, but had moved back into the area about a year before her dad threw her out, so she hadn't got to know him well. But he had a distinctive strawberry birth mark on his right cheek, so he was easy to recognise.

Peter's partner was with him today, she realised: a heavy-set, bearded man whose name was either Colin or Colm. She could never remember which, so dreaded having to address him in case she got it wrong.

'That's right,' she said, digging her hands into her jacket pockets.

'I've not seen you in years.'

'Yes,' she said awkwardly, not really wanting to share her concerns with a virtual stranger, 'I ... I've just dropped in for a surprise visit.'

Peter nodded, a hint of sympathy in his face, as though he knew how difficult her father could be. But if he was still church warden, he had probably run up against her dad's more prickly side on occasion.

'How are you?'

'Fine, thanks.' Stella managed a faint smile for him. 'Don't you have a spare key to the church, Peter?'

He looked embarrassed, as the others glanced at him. 'Yes, I do have a key somewhere. But I've mislaid it.'

'That's a pity.'

She looked round at them all, uncomfortably aware of a strange vibe in the air. The woman in the tweed jacket seemed particularly hostile towards her. But it had been years since she'd been back, and these small rural communities had a tendency to close up behind people once they'd left, never letting them back in. So it was just as well she wasn't back for good, Stella thought.

'Look,' she said, 'I'd better go and see if I can find my dad. But maybe you should think about cancelling the jumble sale? Or perhaps holding it somewhere else?'

Leaving them to discuss this apparently outrageous suggestion, Stella crossed the churchyard to where the oldest headstones stood, their overgrown graves overshadowed by dark-branched wych elms.

There was a large, hulking woman bent over one of the older gravestones, wrapped in a thick anorak and with a woollen beanie pulled down over a shock of unlikely blonde hair.

She half-turned as Stella passed, and grunted something that might have been, 'Good morning.'

She recognised the woman as Fifi Maggs, a local eccentric who had lived in a tent down by the river for years – or had done before Stella left. Maybe she had somewhere more permanent now, though she looked as raggedy as ever, her boots thick with dried mud.

Fifi Maggs was well-known for stalking the church and vicarage grounds in hope of a conversation with whoever happened to be passing, or perhaps just a free cup of tea. Her father humoured Fifi with an occasional chat and biscuits, probably because most people in the area ignored the poor woman and he felt it was his Christian duty not to do the same.

'Hello,' Stella said briefly, unsmiling, and walked on without looking back.

The last thing she wanted right now was to get into conversation with Fifi Maggs, who had a reputation for yelling at people when she was in a bad mood. And the woman didn't look particularly friendly today.

Stella vaulted the low wall that separated the Church of St. Joshua from the vicarage, as easily as she had done since she was a child.

The church might date back to Norman times, but the vicarage was early Victorian, all sash windows and drainpipes, its neglected façade a dingy white. She vaguely remembered the church council shelling out for a fresh paint job soon after they moved in, but that had been over two decades ago now.

Her father had been vicar at St. Joshua's for twenty-three years, so she'd grown up in the shadow of the Norman church, played among the gravestones as a child, and roamed the surrounding countryside on her trusty bike with barely any restrictions. During school holidays, her mum had usually been busy to notice her absence, hosting coffee mornings as the vicar's wife or rehearsing with the local drama group she helped run, and the Reverend Penhaligon himself had been too preoccupied to care, frequently locked up in his private study.

Besides, she had been instantly recognisable everywhere as the vicar's daughter, a badge she had worn not with pride, but a kind of creeping horror. The last thing she'd felt inside was religious or well-behaved.

No doubt she'd been a rebellious child, she thought.

At the time, all she'd registered was a dislike of living under her father's roof and by his rules, and so had not been exactly unhappy when he threw her out after university …

Ignoring the front door, she trod quietly round to the back, fishing in her pocket for her old key. The back door opened easily.

'Hello? Dad?'

The kitchen was tidy, but empty. The fluorescent lights were on despite the daylight, humming away pointlessly. She closed the door behind her, turned off the lights, and wandered into the hall.

'Dad? It's Stella here.' She raised her voice to reach up to the bedrooms, in case he was lying ill in bed. 'Are you in? Can you hear me?'

Total silence greeted her. She stood at the base of the stairs and peered up, her hand on the smooth banister.

The curtains at the top of the stairs were closed, the space in shadow.

Had her father left the house during darkness and not been back since? Or had something happened to prevent him from opening those curtains and turning off the kitchen light?

For a moment she hung motionless, unsure what to do. Then she turned to check the downstairs rooms – both empty and unremarkable – before heading upstairs, dread in her heart.

What was she going to find up there?

His bedroom was empty, the bed covers crumpled, thrown back. Nothing strange there, she had never known her father to make his own bed. Or even to tidy the house.

At one stage, he'd had a cleaner who would come in once a week to take care of things like that, and do a wash of his clerical clothes. But she knew he'd started living more sparingly, as she'd noticed on her last visit here – God, how long ago? Five years? – when the dust in some rooms had been noticeable, and his clothes dishevelled. She'd felt a twinge of guilt, seeing him like that and aware he was alone here, having to fend for himself. Yet he was the one who'd thrown *her* out. She hadn't left.

Now the large vicarage kitchen looked surprisingly clean, and she was pretty sure someone must have hoovered the hall and reception rooms recently. They had been almost presentable.

Had he got another cleaner?

The door to her old bedroom was partially open.

Stella pushed the door, but the room was empty, like all the rest on that floor, including the bathroom.

She went to the window. The blinds were open. Outside, she could see the grey sky and the small back garden of the vicarage, a square of unmown lawn with straggly flowerbeds being gradually overtaken by weeds. His gardening skills hadn't improved, then.

She turned on her heel, looking around slowly. Her old stuff was still in the room: posters on the wall, dusty belongings on shelves, textbooks and teen novels she hadn't bothered to take with her. The bed had been stripped and covered with a single white sheet. Otherwise, it looked untouched.

Six, seven years …

Yet he had never made any effort to use the room for another purpose. Was he hoping she might come back, perhaps? If so, he had never voiced that hope. Barely even contacted her, in fact. So it was more likely to be laziness or apathy. Not affection.

There was only one more place in the house to look.

'Dad?' she called up the narrow stairs to the attic, but there was still no answer. 'Dad, for God's sake … If you're up there, please say something.'

Silence.

The door was probably locked, anyway. The attic stairs were in darkness. When she tried the light switch, nothing happened. Was the bulb broken?

Dad was probably out, she told herself, ready to turn away. Maybe he'd gone away to visit a friend. He must still have one or two friends out there somewhere. She knew he'd had quite a large circle of friends when younger, in the years before becoming a vicar, but had mostly kept to himself since those days. Or maybe he'd been taken ill and was in hospital.

But she was still his next of kin. Wouldn't someone have contacted her if he was sick? Unless he'd told them not to. That would be like him.

'I'm coming up,' she said loudly.

But when she reached the door into the long, low attic room her father used as his private study, she found it already unlocked …

CHAPTER SIX

Jack nodded to the seat opposite, and flipped open his notepad as the woman with long black hair sat down. She was pale, her eyes wide.

'Sorry to keep you waiting so long, Miss Penhaligon. If you could just go over again what you told the desk sergeant …' He gave her an encouraging smile when she stiffened, no doubt bored after hanging about the station for several hours and unwilling to start repeating her story. 'You say your father's gone missing. The Reverend Charles Penhaligon.'

He tried not to smile as he wrote out and underlined the name in his notepad. A missing vicar. Was this really their only lead on the gory head found at Tintagel?

'Church of England vicar, is he?'

'Yes.'

'Are you sure he hasn't gone on holiday or to visit someone?'

'I'm sure,' Miss Penhaligon said firmly.

'What makes you so sure?'

'Well, for starters, his private study's been trashed. I went to the house this morning – the vicarage – and when I went up to his study, it was a complete mess. All his drawers open, papers and books everywhere, glass cabinets smashed.' She hesitated, looking uncertain, as though trying not to reveal too much. It was a look that immediately made him suspicious. But about what, exactly? 'Also, some of his most prize possessions are missing.'

He sat back, considering her with sudden interest. A break-in, theft, and a missing man. This sounded more like a possible ringer for their decapitated head.

'His study. What about the rest of the house?'

'Untouched.' Miss Penhaligon hesitated. 'As far as I know, anyway. It looked fairly tidy. Carpets hoovered. Kitchen clean.'

'So only his study was targeted? Wait, you said, prized possessions?' A possible motive occurred to him. 'Do you mean valuables?'

'I don't know about value. He's a collector of … ' She paused. 'Well, I'm not quite sure about that either. Arcane objects.'

'And when did you last see him?'

'Five years, maybe?'

Jack glanced up at her, surprised. 'Why so long? And what took you to the vicarage today?'

'This.'

She turned her phone screen on and pushed the mobile towards him. It was a text message. *Give me a ring, I need to speak to you urgently.* He glanced at the date stamp. She had answered it, but not for several days. Not a close relationship, then. *Five years.* He studied her cool face and wondered again what had caused the estrangement. If that was what it was.

Out of habit, he reached for his own phone and took a photograph of the message exchange on her screen.

'So, what about your mother? Where does she fit into all this?'

'She left him years ago. Lives in London. I … I can give you her address, if you like.'

'That would be helpful. So you told my colleague that the church was locked. That it hasn't been open since last Sunday's service, in fact. Is that right?'

'That's what I was told, yes.'

She started to explain, in a quiet, matter-of-fact way, how the church operated, the kind of public events hosted there, and how she had arrived on Friday morning to find some disgruntled locals on the scene, unable to get inside for their monthly jumble sale.

Jack nodded and watched her face, her body language, listened to the strain in her voice behind the calm explanation. She was good at hiding her feelings. But every now and then her voice would crack, or her mouth grimace, or her eyes fly to the door or wall clock in obvious anxiety.

She was worried. That was a given. Her father, a respectable vicar in late middle age, was missing and his study had been turned over.

But was she also hiding something?

He could not understand why anyone would want to murder a vicar and trash his study. Let alone decapitate him. But they had no other recent reports of missing persons, and the area certainly fitted, his vicarage situated only a few miles up the north coast from Tintagel. It was worth considering at least. Perhaps Reverend Penhaligon had owned something worth stealing.

But stealing was one thing. Grim, ritualistic murder quite another. No, there would have to be more to this puzzle for the pieces to fit.

Still, he hesitated over his next question, not particularly wanting to ask this woman to look at the grisly head they'd found. Especially if it turned out to be her father.

But there was no other option.

Besides, it was common for murderers to be related to the victim. So he had to keep an open mind about this one. He couldn't imagine anything more incongruous than the idea of the pale, composed woman opposite him sawing off her own father's head and then displaying it on a weather-worn windowsill in Tintagel Castle. But he had seen stranger things in his time.

'Miss Penhaligon,' he said, before correcting that to a gentler, 'Stella,' and clearing his throat, 'I have some potentially bad news for you.'

'Oh God.'

'It may not be relevant. But we did recently find some, erm, remains. A little further up the coast from your father's vicarage.'

'*Remains?*'

He nodded. 'I wouldn't have mentioned it, but I'm afraid they match the physical description you gave us of your father.' Her dark eyes widened, fixed on his face, but she said nothing. 'Would you feel up to taking a look, Stella? I'm sure there's no connection to your father, but we do need to be sure.' He could see horror in her face now. 'If you can't face it, I'll perfectly understand.'

'No, no, I'll … do it.'

Her hands twisted on the table top. A silver ring glinted on her hand. The right, he noted. Not an engagement or wedding ring, then. Long slim fingers, slender wrists. She wore hardly any jewellery, only stud earrings and a silver chain with pendant. The design looked like a pentagram. Rather exotic for a vicar's daughter, he thought. And she was wearing all black.

'You … You think he's dead, then?' she asked.

'I don't think anything, Miss Penhaligon. It's early days yet. At this stage, I prefer to keep an open mind.'

'But you still want me to look at these … remains?'

'Just to eliminate it from our enquiries.'

'I can show you a photo.'

'No need. I've already taken a quick look online.'

'And it matches?'

'There are definite similarities. But a personal ID by a relative still has to be done. It's a formality. I apologise.'

She nodded, and then looked away, her mouth tightening. 'I suppose it would make sense.'

'Sorry, what would?'

'His text message.' She nodded to the phone, still on his side of the table. 'It sounded so urgent, and then … He didn't answer any of my calls or reply to my texts.'

'You appear to have waited a while before coming to us.'

'We're not close.' Her mouth twisted. 'Besides, I thought Dad was just being bloody-minded. He often is with me.'

'I see.' He looked again at the black-etched pentagram on its silver chain. 'Differences of opinion?'

'Something like that.'

'But you think it makes sense for him to be *dead*?'

Her gaze lifted to his face. He read confusion in her face, but no pretence. 'Only because he didn't call. This body you want me to see. Was it … Was it a heart attack? Was he out walking?'

'Did he go in for that much? Walking, I mean?'

'He liked to be out in nature. He said it helped him to think. Sometimes he would … '

'Go on.'

'Sometimes he used to go out for walks at night.' She frowned. 'But only locally. In the woods near the church. Or down by the river.' She looked at him directly as though trying to gauge his reaction. 'Maybe he … had an accident. Walking at night.'

'Thank you for agreeing to view the deceased,' was all he said, deliberately not responding to her probing. 'Is right now okay?'

She nodded, looking stressed.

'I'll set it up straightaway.' Jack closed the notepad.

'I'd prefer to get it over with.' She reached for her phone, and he let her take it back, though they might need it as evidence if the remains turned out to be her missing father. 'I don't want to sound callous, Detective Sergeant Church, but I can't believe it will be him.'

'Of course not.' He hesitated. 'Call me Jack, please.'

'Jack.' She gave him a thin, utterly unconvincing smile. 'I know this must seem awful at a time like this, but will this take long? I have … work to get back to.'

'Naturally,' he said soothingly. 'If you wait here, I'll arrange the viewing. We should be back here by about two o'clock.'

'Thank you.'

'What do you do, by the way?'

Her gaze was suddenly defiant, almost cold. 'I'm an astrologer.'

'Interesting.'

'A professional astrologer. I read people's birth charts for a living.'

'I get it.'

Stella Penhaligon stood abruptly, as though planning to leave despite his previous instruction to wait.

'That's why we fell out in the end. Me and Dad. He hated what I was doing, you see.' She jerked to a halt, a faint flush in her cheeks, and then took a deep breath. 'He called me a witch.'

Jack stood too.

Light had finally dawned for him. The sinister pentagram around her neck. The odd hesitations when speaking of her vicar father. The delay in responding to his 'urgent' message. Her uncomfortable demeanour throughout this interview.

Daddy hadn't liked her chosen career, and his rebellious daughter hadn't given a toss. Or not enough to jack it in for something more respectable. Or maybe she had zeroed in on astrology deliberately, to spite her father.

'That must have been hard,' he said.

Her sharp gaze narrowed on his face, and for the first time Jack felt he was seeing the real Stella Penhaligon. 'You don't know the half of it.'

CHAPTER SEVEN

Stella's mouth was dry, her hands trembling, an ache in the pit of her stomach. She focused on the fair sheen of DS Church's head a few feet away, his tall figure stooping as he spoke to the mortuary attendant. What was he? Six foot two? Six three? The detective was skinny too, like he didn't eat enough. Or perhaps had been ill recently. He had sad eyes, she thought. And not just because he'd been telling her that her missing father might, in fact, be dead.

She listened to the slight hum from the overhead lights and the large fridge against the back wall of the mortuary. But they could only distract her for so long from the horror of this moment.

Behind her, she could hear voices from the reception area they had passed through, the incongruous sound of laughter, and a telephone ringing.

Life went on, she thought.

People died every day, some in their beds, others in the most horrible and incomprehensible of ways.

The world continued without so much as a hiccup.

A planetary aspect hit the natal chart.

The planets swept past without pausing, unmoved by consequences major or minor, following the dictates of a deeper, more powerful pattern.

It was left to people like her to stop and think.

To grieve.

Was she grieving, though? Was this trembling grief or was it merely shock and bewilderment?

She had not cried, after all.

Yet.

Perhaps it wouldn't be her father, though. Perhaps it would be some other man instead. A complete stranger. Perhaps her father had simply gone on holiday, as the detective had suggested. That would make more sense.

'A head,' he'd told her on the way over, when it was too late for her to change her mind about identifying the remains.

'*A head*? Th-That's all you found?' She had been appalled, unprepared for such a grim disclosure. 'You mean, somebody – '

'Removed it, yes.'

'Oh my God.' She had struggled to understand, and given up. 'But what makes you think - ?'

'It matches his photos. I'm sorry.'

That was all they had found.

A head.

She didn't think she could do this. But she was here now, in the bloody room. She had to go through with it. To face it. Whatever this was.

DS Church was talking in a low voice to the mortuary attendant with the clipboard, whose name she had not caught when he introduced her. The man, wearing a white plastic apron over blue overalls, looked at her pityingly over the sergeant's shoulder, and nodded.

'Over here,' he said, and led them both through to a smaller room, its pristine floors and walls both tiled, lighting more muted, and closed the door behind them as though for added privacy.

Abruptly, the sounds from the reception area ceased, locking the three of them in a tense, soft-soled silence.

There was a shape on a high table, draped in blue cloth.

She halted, not wanting to move any closer.

There was a horrible stench in the air. The stink of death. Something rotting, she thought. And something else. The faint hint of patchouli oil. Her father would use it sometimes on his beard. 'Old habits die hard,' he used to say, dabbing it on. Her mother had told her once that he'd been a bit of a New Age hippy back in the day. Before the church beckoned.

Bile rose in her throat.

DS Church looked round at her, frowning. 'You okay? Do you still want to do this?'

'Yes,' she lied.

The two men waited beside the discreetly draped shape until she came closer, then DS Church nodded. The mortuary attendant lifted the blue cloth slowly and deliberately, watching her expression, like a magician revealing the outcome of a trick to a stunned audience.

Stella reeled back like she'd been struck in the face, wrenching her horrified gaze away and turning her back on them.

'Yes,' she gasped, clamping a hand to her mouth. 'That's him. That's my father.' She gulped several times. 'I'm sorry, but I think … '

Suddenly, the man in the white plastic apron was beside her, holding out a thick cardboard basin. 'Here.'

Stella jerked the basin to her mouth and retched over it several times, her shoulders shaking. It was not pleasant. But then, what she'd seen under the blue cloth had not been pleasant either. And, judging by the understanding silence from the two men, her reaction was not wholly unexpected.

The man took the basin in a matter-of-fact way and handed her some blue paper hand towels from a dispenser on the wall.

'Thank you,' she managed to say. 'Sorry.'

'No need to apologise. It's quite common in cases like this.' He pointed out a bin near the sink. 'For the used towels.'

The man rustled out of the room with the basin, leaving her alone with DS Church. And what remained of her father.

'You okay?' he asked again, frowning.

She thrust the soiled towels in the bin, drank a little cold water from the tap over the sink, rinsed out her mouth, and then washed and dried her hands.

Caput Algol.

The malevolent pulsating star on top of her father's Sun in Taurus, that had been triggered by an otherwise harmless transit. She had read about it years ago. Caput Algol was said to resemble a severed head, and in a close conjunction was associated with witchcraft and death by violent means, including hanging, electrocution … *and decapitation.*

DS Church was looking at her in a concerned way.

Stella said, 'It was a shock, that's all. I'm … I'm better now.'

'Of course.'

'Have you found …. '

'The rest of him?' The detective shook his head. 'But we do have people out looking. It's only a matter of time.'

She shuddered, pushing away the thought of Caput Algol, the Demon Star. It had to be a coincidence, didn't it? She didn't really believe in all that ancient Arabian stuff about fixed stars and their influence …

'Look, do you mind if we get out of here?' The head had been covered again, but the stench was still in her nostrils. Stella couldn't bring herself to look in that direction again. 'It's definitely him.'

'Thank you.' DS Church led her back towards reception, and sat down beside her in the waiting area. 'I know you must be in shock,' he said calmly, studying her face. 'But this is a very serious crime, and we urgently need to catch whoever is responsible. Which means I need to ask you some questions straightway, even if the timing feels a bit … indelicate.'

She nodded silently, staring down at her hands.

At least she'd stopped trembling.

'First, I have to ask, do you have any idea who might have done that to your father, and why?'

'No.'

'Did he have any enemies?'

'My father is … ' She stopped with a painful jolt, and corrected herself. 'He *was* a vicar. Why on earth would he have enemies?'

'I'm sorry, but I have to ask questions like that.' The detective sergeant took out his pen and notepad again, finding the right page and studying his notes. 'Your father and mother are separated, is that right?'

'Divorced.'

He scribbled something. 'And she lives in London.'

'East London. She has family there. That's why she went back after … after they split up.'

'And how do they get on now?'

Stella shrugged helplessly. 'They don't. As far as I know.'

'Meaning?'

'I'm not aware of either of them contacting the other since Mum left,' she said, surprised. 'Why would they?'

'So it didn't end amicably?'

'Of course not. How many marriages end amicably?' Turning her head, Stella stared at him suspiciously. 'Why all these questions about my mum? For God's sake, you can't imagine my mother would come here all the way from London, after all these years, to do something … something like *that*?' Firmly, she pushed aside the appalling image of her father's decapitated head. 'That's sick.'

'I'm just trying to get a picture of your father's life. His relationships. Past and present.' He paused. 'Did he have any?'

'Any what?'

'Current relationships?'

'I have no idea.'

'No girlfriend? Partner? Nobody at all?'

'I told you, we weren't close. I hadn't been in contact with him for some years. But I don't think … ' She frowned, remembering how tidy the vicarage had seemed downstairs.

DS Church was watching her closely. 'What is it?'

'It did strike me how clean the vicarage was, compared to how he used to keep it. I wondered if he'd got a cleaner.' She paused as he scribbled in his notepad again. 'Or a girlfriend, I suppose. Which is horribly sexist, I know. But Dad was never one for hoovering, and someone had definitely hoovered downstairs. Unlikely to be a male friend, I suppose.'

'Sorry for asking this, but your father was straight, I take it?'

'Very.'

He looked at her sharply. 'What does that mean?'

'Dad had some old-fashioned views about sexuality. But he always towed the line as far as the church was concerned. When they got more relaxed about gay marriage, he did too.' She grimaced, remembering some of her father's more strident rants against homosexuality. His intolerance for anyone 'different' had been one of the reasons she had been only too happy to leave home, never quite able to fall in line with his strict views and beliefs. 'Though frankly, I'm not sure how deep that went.'

'Lip service only, then?'

'Probably.'

More scribbling in his notepad.

'And you can't think of any enemies he might have made?'

'I told you, we weren't that close.' Stella shivered, suddenly feeling cold. 'Perhaps you should talk to Peter Harbut. He's one of the church wardens. He and Dad would probably have worked together quite closely over the past few years. If anyone knows whether Dad had a girlfriend or … or any enemies, Peter would.'

She gave him Peter's address and he wrote it down.

'How long do you think it will take before … before you find the … ' Stella choked on the words. 'His remains?' She fumbled for what was appropriate in a situation like this. 'I suppose I'll need to make arrangements for his funeral.'

'As this is a murder enquiry, I'm afraid a funeral is out of the question for now.' DS Church closed his notepad. 'But finding your father's remains is our top priority. Hopefully, it won't be too long.'

'It's horrible, thinking of him somewhere out there, undiscovered.'

'We'll do our best.'

She stood up, suddenly aware of a pressing need to be alone. 'I have to go home.'

'Of course.' DS Church led her out to the car park. 'We may need your phone at some point.'

'My phone?'

'He sent you that message, remember?'

'Oh, right.'

'I took a photograph of his message, and your replies. But we may need to look at the original at some point. So please don't delete those messages.'

'Of course.'

'Meanwhile, if you think of anything else that might help our enquiries, anything at all.' He handed her a card. 'My number's there. Call me any time.'

She got back home for half past three, not surprised to find the house empty. Julie and Claire frequently went straight to the pub after school finished on a Friday, and Nick would be at work for at least another hour. Stella went straight upstairs to her room and turned on her computer, thankful not to encounter any of her fellow housemates. She was not feeling up to explaining what had happened today; she felt more like crawling under the covers and hiding, in fact.

But what possible good would denial do?

All the way home, she had been thinking, why would anyone want her father dead? He had been a reverend, a harmless vicar, a man of the cloth. And not just that, why in God's name would anyone choose not only to murder him, but decapitate him and then hide or possibly scatter the rest of his body?

It was unspeakably horrible.

And it made no sense.

She could possibly have understood the body being left in the open while the head was concealed, but not the other way around.

Whoever had done this had clearly not been trying to hide her father's identity or slow down the police in identifying their victim. His head had been left out in the open for all to see. As though on public display, from the way the sergeant had described it to her on the way to the police morgue. There had to be a reason. But what was it? And where was the rest of his body?

The whole thing was a riddle, and one she had no hope of solving.

It also made her feel sick again, just thinking about it.

The one useful thought in her head was that she might be able to answer at least one of those questions with astrology.

There was an ancient branch of astrology called 'horary'. Its rules of interpretation tended to be strict, following traditionally established guidelines, but allowed room for an astrologer's intuition. She used horary astrology quite frequently to answer specific questions some of her clients might pose, including the location of missing objects.

Missing objects.

Like what remained of her father?

She groaned.

It seemed inappropriate to ask such a thing of the universe, and certainly indelicate. But it was worth a try. His murderer had clearly gone to some trouble to conceal her father's body, while flaunting his head for all the world to see. So if she left it to the police alone, it could be weeks before they found the rest of him. Assuming they ever did.

With that question firmly in mind – 'Where are my father's remains?' – Stella opened her astrological software, brought up a chart of current planetary transits to her location in Cornwall, and began to study it.

CHAPTER EIGHT

'This place is a right mess, sarge. I wonder what he was looking for?'

'*He*?'

'Or they, I guess.' Ronny glanced at him. 'You're thinking more than one person was involved in this?'

'I'm not sure what I'm thinking. I try not to think too much at this stage, only look.'

'Right.' Ronny sounded dubious. No doubt his constable never had trouble thinking 'too much'.

Jack nudged a heap of torn and tumbled papers with his foot. Loose papers were everywhere in the Reverend Penhaligon's attic study, which appeared to have been some kind of inner sanctum for the vicar. Strange diagrams on what looked like faded parchment. Entire sheets written in Latin, others in Greek. Some in what might be Hebrew, but there his linguistic skills failed him.

The vicarage room had been thoroughly turned over, folders and boxes emptied out, books thrown about, drawers searched.

But what, as Ronny had said, had the killer, or killers plural, been looking for up here? The ferocity and wildness of the debris left behind – glass cabinets smashed, pictures slashed, books and papers ripped up – suggested both vindictiveness and urgency. Though there was also a good chance this mess was designed to throw them off the scent, concealing the true purpose of their visit.

The theft of something valuable, perhaps. Or the retrieval of something incriminating.

Perhaps both at the same time.

'What the hell did he use this for, do you suppose?' With a tissue, Ronny held up a grinning bleached sheep's skull and turned it towards Jack. 'What kind of vicar keeps a skull about the place?'

'Or a jewelled dagger?' Jack reached into the one cabinet that had been left unbroken and, using an evidence bag to avoid destroying potential evidence, removed the short, black-handled knife inset with a reddish gem of some kind. 'This looks … ceremonial.'

'This too.' Ronny was frowning into the skull, which appeared to have a large hole bored in its cranium. 'There's been a candle stuck in this. Black wax.'

Jack studied the diagram of a black-edged pentagram on the wall. There was an inscription underneath in Latin. Something about the moon?

Ex luna scientia.

The moon … and something to do with science. No, *from* the moon science. Or knowledge. *We get knowledge from the moon*?

He grimaced at his fumbling translation; he'd studied Latin at school, but eventually dropped it in favour of French. Ordering a train ticket in Paris had seemed a more useful skill to have than knowing what Caesar had told his troops before some obscure Roman battle.

Whatever it meant, it didn't sound very religious. Or not the sort of religion a vicar ought to be promoting.

'Definitely something not right here. No wonder he kept this room under lock and key.' Jack slipped the dagger into the evidence bag and sealed it. 'Do you get the feeling the Reverend Penhaligon wasn't strictly Church of England?'

'What? Black magic shit?'

'Maybe.'

'Did you manage to contact the ex-wife in London?'

'Yes, sarge.'

'And?'

'Solid alibi. She's been at work every day, including last Sunday. Some kind of market stall. Says the other stall holders can confirm if necessary. Plus, there's a CCTV camera near her stall.'

'So she's out of the frame, at least.'

Ronny shrugged. 'Unless she put someone else up to it.'

'You've got a suspicious mind, constable.'

'And in any other job, sarge, that might be a problem.'

Jack grinned, but did not reply. His young constable, new to the ways of CID, was prone to informality, which was okay when DI Martin wasn't around. The inspector was a stickler for the rules, and came down hard on younger officers who didn't do things strictly according to the book. Jack himself was more relaxed about such things. But if he encouraged it too much, it could get them both in trouble. Not to mention becoming an issue when he urgently needed something done and DC Myles decided to ignore him, for whatever reason. Which did seem to happen rather more often than he liked.

He picked up the swivel chair and set it back behind the desk, then sat down carefully and studied the drawers. All four desk drawers had been dragged open, their contents in complete disarray, some littering the floor below. One printed sheet was poking out of a torn folder.

He removed the sheet and cast his eye over it.

'What's that, sarge?'

'Bank statements, looks like.' Jack opened the folder and thumbed slowly through the other sheets. 'Personal though, not to do with the church.' He paused, frowning. 'Now, that's odd.'

'Something useful?'

Ronny came across to read over his shoulder, an old, leather-bound volume in his hand.

'There's a payment here to a P. A. Harbut. Rather a large payment.' Jack folded the sheet in two, then two again, and placed it carefully inside his notebook. 'Thirty thousand pounds.'

Ronny whistled. 'What's that about, then, do you reckon?'

'I remember that name. Peter Harbut. One of the church wardens. Stella Penhaligon gave me his name, to check on the Rev's recent movements, but I haven't been in touch with him yet.'

'Is he a builder? Maybe the Rev needed some work done and this Harbut bloke did it for him. An extension, maybe.'

'Could be, I suppose,' Jack agreed. 'Though I haven't seen any sign of new work being done about the place.'

'An advance payment, then?'

'For so much? That seems unlikely.' Jack looked through the bank statements, some of them going back several years, but couldn't find any other mention of that name. 'Besides, who charges thirty grand on the nose? Not single pounds or pence. Just a cool thirty thousand. Strikes me as a bit odd.' He paused. 'Dodgy, even.'

'Now you put it like that, it does feel suspicious.'

'Something for you to chase up, then. Get me a phone number and address.'

'Yes, sarge.'

Jack glanced at the book in the constable's hand. The red leather spine and cover both displayed the same arcane-looking lettering and a curious symbol like a black star.

'What have you found there? More black magic?'

Ronny nodded. 'Lodged down the back of one of them wall cabinets. Like it was hidden, not there accidentally.'

'You think it could be what they were looking for?'

'Possible, I guess. Though I doubt it's worth much. Just some kind of old journal.' Ronny showed him the book, flicking through the pages. Some were dated and handwritten in black spidery ink. Others had newspaper or magazine cuttings stuck in, or dried flowers pressed between the pages, like a scrapbook. 'On the other hand, I don't imagine the Rev would have wanted people to know about his little side hobby. Not surprised he kept this hidden. It's a blackmailer's dream.' Ronny raised his eyebrows, studying one of the pages. 'Jesus!'

'What is it?'

'Some dark stuff in here about magic and rituals and so on.' The constable turned to the cover, reading its title aloud, '*Book of Shadows*. Doesn't sound too cheery, does it?'

'Well, take it back to headquarters, I'll have a closer look later. Plus all the other stuff we've bagged. Then I'll drive over to speak to Peter Harbut.'

'Right you are.'

'Meanwhile, I want to have a quick look around the rest of the house. I presume there was nothing interesting in any of the downstairs rooms?'

Ronny shook his head. 'Clean as a whistle, sarge.'

He left the constable bagging and gathering the evidence together, and went back down to the first floor bedrooms. He had taken a quick look around them before heading up to the attic study, but he wanted a chance to examine *her* room more thoroughly. Stella Penhaligon's room. Or what he guessed must have been her bedroom when she still lived here at the vicarage.

Jack wandered into her former bedroom, gazing about the place without really knowing what he was looking for.

No effort had been made to box up her things or change the décor since her departure, as far as he could see. Not had whoever was responsible for cleaning up downstairs bothered to come in here. There were dusty posters on the wall and educational textbooks on the bookshelves, along with an array of teen and young adult fiction. Romances and fantasy novels, mostly. He had read some of the fantasy titles as a lad himself.

He pulled out one of the old paperbacks, part of a series about a teen witch, and raised his eyebrows, reading the unlikely blurb on the back.

She'd lived here as an adult too, not just as a child. But hadn't got rid of these books. Maybe Stella Penhaligon had read too much fantasy and it had affected her brain. By the age of fifteen, he'd started to move onto adult thrillers and spy stories, leaving all that kids' stuff behind.

I'm an astrologer. I read people's birth charts for a living.

Not as a hobby or out of amateur interest. *For a living.* She had stressed that, as though she was proud of that.

An unusual profession, astrology.

Like being a medium.

She hadn't struck him as a dishonest person. But astrology? Birth charts? That kind of nonsense was no more true than tarot or psychic readings, all of them intended to fleece the superstitious and unwary.

The woman was selling snake oil. Had to be. Unless she believed all that New Age claptrap herself. Which no sensible person could, surely?

He thought of her pale face, her expressive eyes. The tilt of her head as she'd looked him over. Consideringly, as though trying to work him out.

She'd seemed sensible enough.

And her visceral response on seeing her father's decapitated head had satisfied him that Stella Penhaligon had nothing to do with his murder. Not unless she was the best actor he had ever encountered. Plus being able to throw up to order.

No, there was nothing out of the ordinary here, he thought, replacing the book and turning to leave. Except that something was still nagging at him about Stella Penhaligon. Something he couldn't put his finger on.

Clean as a whistle.

She'd said something like that in her interview, hadn't she? Stella, the astrologer, the vicar's daughter. She'd said the house was tidier than she'd anticipated. As though somebody – and not her father, who'd been a bit of a slob, at least by her account – had gone around the downstairs of the vicarage with a duster and a vacuum cleaner. Why?

To remove forensic evidence, was his first thought.

But if that was the case, why make a big effort to tidy downstairs only to leave the trashed attic room in such a state?

CHAPTER NINE

Stella badly needed to share her new findings with someone trustworthy before approaching the police with it. Not to mention the grim news about her father. But Claire and Julie were still both out, and she had a feeling they'd mentioned a meal out together after the pub. So there'd be no help from that quarter tonight.

When Nick got home from his Friday shift at the care home, she waited for him to shower and change into his civvies, then asked if he could spare her a few minutes in her room.

Nick listened to her story about her father, the decapitated head the police had found, and how she had identified it, and his eyes slowly widened as the horrible story unfolded. She even showed him the horary chart she'd drawn up to find the rest of her father's remains, still up on the screen behind her.

'Jesus, Stella, I'm so sorry.' Nick ran a hand through slick, shower-damp hair. 'Who the hell could have that done something like to your dad? To a vicar, for God's sake? I mean, I'm not religious myself, but all the same. That's pretty nasty.'

'I know, it doesn't bear thinking about … you know, what he must have suffered.'

'If there's anything I can do.' Nick gave her an awkward hug, still smelling of citrus shower gel. 'You look like you need a stiff drink, frankly.'

'I've had better days.'

'We've got some brandy in the kitchen. You want a glass?'

'Not yet. I need to keep my head straight. But thank you.'

'I think I could do with one,' he said, grimacing. 'But what about this chart you've drawn up? The hor … Whatever it's called?'

'Horary. It means to do with hours.' Stella angled the computer screen round to show him the chart. 'Horary astrology is used to answer a specific question, usually yes/no. You look for positive or negative signifiers, and depending on how many of each you find, and how strong they are, that gives you a basic yes or no answer.

But, in this case, it's more complicated, because I'm asking about the location of a missing item.'

Nick frowned. 'And who are you asking?'

'The universe, I guess. Or the chart itself. It doesn't really matter who we're asking or how it works, only that it does, in my experience. So I suppose you have to take it on faith. But quite a lot of life is like that, isn't it? Taking things on faith.' Stella took a deep breath, studying the complex horary chart on the screen, which she knew would be just a collection of symbols, squiggles and coloured lines to Nick. 'Anyway, I asked the universe where my dad's remains are. I mean, where the … the rest of him is.'

When she shuddered, Nick put a reassuring hand on her shoulder. 'I get it. And what does the chart say?'

'Well,' she said reluctantly, 'it's a bit unclear.'

'Why am I not surprised?'

'Hey, this stuff really works!' She stuck her tongue out at him, and he laughed. 'Though it can be infuriatingly vague at times, I have to admit.'

'Let's hear the vagueness, then.'

'Okay, it says we need to look relatively nearby, somewhere with water and woods, maybe in a valley or a cave of some kind. Probably somewhere dark and damp. Also, there's some kind of ritual attached to the place.'

'How the hell does a chart say all that?'

She smiled. 'Okay, you want a quick lesson in horary astrology? See this here?' Stella pointed to one of the astrological symbols on the screen, the one that she always thought looked like the number 4, only drawn more loosely. 'That's the symbol for Jupiter.'

'Roman king of the gods?'

'That's right. I've taken Jupiter to signify my father, because it's the planet that rules priests and spiritual matters, and he was a vicar.'

'Go on.'

'Jupiter is in the twelfth, approaching the Ascendant. The twelfth is a house of invisible things, and also prisons, large institutions.'

'So he's hidden?'

'Exactly.' She tapped the screen. 'He's hidden, but not far away, because of how close Jupiter is to the Ascendant. So I'm taking that to mean he's probably close to me, as the person asking the question. Hence, not far away.'

'Okay, I can see how that works out. But the rest?'

'Capricorn is on the Ascendant. That sign is ruled by Saturn, so Saturn is Lord One.'

'Hold on, Lord what?'

'Lord One.' She made a face, realising this was probably too complicated for him to understand in a few minutes' conversation. 'It means, the planet that rules the first house in the chart. Lord One is also the chart ruler. So it's likely to be highly significant in a missing person chart.'

'And which one is Saturn?'

'This squiggly symbol here, in the first house.'

'That odd-looking thing?' Nick peered at the astrological sigil for Saturn. 'Looks like a wheelchair sign.'

Stella rolled her eyes at him. 'Sensitively put, as always, Nick. But yes, I suppose it does a bit.'

'And what does that tell us?'

'Plenty,' she said unhappily. 'So Saturn is the chart ruler, as well as the natural ruler of the tenth house of the father, and here it's conjunct Pluto, planet of death. My father is dead.' A sensation of coldness washed through her at the icy finality of those words. 'Okay, that much we know. But where is his body?'

'You said woods or water or something?'

'Saturn is in its natural home of Capricorn, an earth sign, and conjunct Pluto, god of the underworld. That suggests a dark earthy place to me, woods maybe, or a cave. Somewhere low down, for sure. But then there's the Moon.' She tapped the crescent symbol in the second house. 'She also rules missing objects, so we have to take her position into account too.'

'Oh, I can see how that's the Moon. That's an easy symbol.'

'The Moon is in the second house of values, in the water sign of Pisces. To me, that says, also look near water.'

'Water?'

'I don't know. The sea? A river? A pond, even.'

'I get it.'

'And because it's in the second house of values, probably somewhere that meant something special to him. A place that he valued.' She paused, frowning. 'Or perhaps a place I value, as the one drawing up the chart. Hard to be sure.'

'Did you say the tenth house was connected to your dad too?'

'It rules parents. The fourth can be a parent too. But here … ' She looked broodingly at the tenth house. 'I'd say that's definitely my dad. Scorpio on the tenth cusp. Authoritative, powerful, but also dark and secretive, good at concealing things. He's actually a Taurean, but he has a strong Pluto in his chart, and Pluto rules Scorpio in modern astrology.' She paused, thinking out loud, 'Plus, Lord Ten is in the Eleventh here. That's potentially interesting.'

Nick scratched his head, studying the chart over her shoulder, and then cleared his throat when she looked round at him. 'Yeah, I totally agree. That's *very* interesting.'

'You have no idea what I'm talking about, do you?'

'You got me. So, what does it mean? Lord Ten … something.'

'Lord Ten means ruler of the tenth house. Here, that's Scorpio, which is ruled by Mars in ancient astrology.' She pointed. 'And see, Mars is in the eleventh house of friends and groups.'

'Which means …'

'Which means this has something to do with friends and groups.' Stella was perplexed. 'It's almost as though the chart is saying his body is … with them.'

'With his friends?'

'Maybe.'

Nick grimaced. 'Seriously?'

'I know, it doesn't make a lot of sense to me either.' Stella sat back, unable to work it out. 'So maybe I'm wrong. Maybe Mars isn't significant here.'

'You're the expert.'

'I wouldn't exactly call myself an expert.' She shifted guiltily. 'I've only been doing this a few years. There are some astrologers out there who could probably read this chart in ten seconds and lead me straight to him.'

'So let's ask them.'

Stella glared at him. 'Apart from the cost, I'd really like to work this out on my own. He was my father. I should be the one to find him.'

'Okay, don't bite my head off.' Nick gave her a wary smile. 'So, what about the ritual element you mentioned?'

She nodded, turning back to the chart. 'Jupiter, my father's significator, is nearing the Ascendant. Planet of rituals and spiritual practice. Also woods or trees again.'

'Hang on, I'm having an idea.' His brows drew together. 'Somewhere that meant something special to him, you said.'

'Or to me. Or both of us.'

'Plus, it has to be somewhere dark and woody, and maybe low down, and probably near water too.'

'That's about the gist of it.'

Nick sucked in a breath, then let it out slowly. 'St. Nectan's Glen.'

'Sorry?'

'St. Nectan's Glen.' He looked at her. 'Visitors leave offerings beside the waterfall there, don't they? Candles, flowers, ribbons, fairy stacks of stones … That kind of thing.'

'They're called votives. Prayers to the Genius Loci, or god of the place.' She shrugged. 'Or to St. Nectan or St. Piran, one of the two. They're both closely connected to that area. So what?'

'So it's a place connected to rituals, like you said.'

'Jupiter ...' She studied the chart again. 'Yes, that would fit. Pretty well, actually. But special to him?'

'Didn't you tell me that your dad used to take you for walks after church on a Sunday, back when you were a kid? And that his favourite place to go walking was St. Nectan's Glen. I'm sure I remember that.' Nick clicked his fingers, clearly excited now. 'You even went back there last year. You said, it felt weird being down in the glen alone, without your dad.'

Stella was astonished by his memory. 'That's right, I did.'

'Not bad after a ten-hour shift, huh? We make a good team. Plus, it's not far from here. Fifteen minutes by car, I reckon.' Nick was still grinning, but sobered up quickly at her expression. 'So, if your horary chart is correct, and we've guessed the right place, that means …'

'My dad's body is hidden somewhere in St. Nectan's Glen, yes.'

CHAPTER TEN

It turned out that P. A. Harbut was no dodgy builder but a local accountant, and a highly respectable one at that.

'Detective Sergeant Church?'

Tall and lanky in a smart but understated black suit, with a fair thatch reminiscent of Boris Johnson's mop, Peter Harbut was in fact a senior partner at the long-established Pethporro firm of Harbut, Tottle & Sons, which had its current premises next to the Co-op on the High Street. The polar opposite of dodgy, he looked like someone who came in early and left late, ate healthily and visited the gym three times a week.

The only striking thing about the man was a facial strawberry birth mark. Not the easiest thing to cope with growing up, Jack thought, shaking his hand. 'Good of you to see me on such short notice, Mr Harbut.'

'Not at all, sergeant. We've actually closed for the day, so I had no more appointments.' Harbut paused a little uncomfortably, then added, 'Your constable said you need help with enquiries into a local incident?'

'That's right, Mr Harbut.'

'I'm not sure how I can help, but I'll do my best.' Harbut dismissed his hovering secretary – a skinny young man in an ill-fitting suit – with a smile, and waved Jack into his office, P.A. Harbut inscribed in gold on the glass panel. 'Please, call me Peter. And take a seat.'

'Thank you.'

Jack did not sit, however, instead prowling the small office with his hands behind his back. He did not often get into Pethporro, and had never had occasion to deal with this particular accountancy firm before.

Traffic rumbled past on the High Street outside while he studied the various plaques, professional awards, and photographs on the walls, finally halting before a shot of Peter Harbut and the Reverend Penhaligon outside the Church of St. Joshua.

The two men were standing in front of the church porch, smiling benignly for the camera, while Peter Harbut held up an outsized cheque made out to the church fund. The photograph was dated underneath: five years ago. The cheque was for three thousand, seven hundred and twenty-two pounds. A pretty impressive amount, Jack thought. But nowhere near the thirty thousand pay-out he'd seen on the Reverend Penhaligon's bank statement.

Peter Harbut came to stand behind him. 'Ah yes,' he said, a sudden note of caution in his voice, 'St. Joshua's.'

'Fund raising?'

'There was a sports and fun day in the field behind the church. To raise money for the upkeep of the church. Such an expensive business with these ancient buildings, there's always something falling apart or rotting away. Most of the surrounding villages took part, as I recall, as did many from Pethporro. Locals and visitors alike. That photograph was used in the local paper. I still have the clipping somewhere.'

'Looks like you raised quite a lot of money.'

'Yes, a pretty good haul.' Harbut sank both hands into his trouser pockets. 'Though our firm made a modest contribution too. We've always supported the Church of St. Joshua in times of need.'

'Why's that?'

'Family tradition.' Harbut studied the photograph too, smiling faintly. 'My father's first name was Joshua, like the saint to whom the church is dedicated. He and his brother founded this firm back in the fifties. I imagine they thought it would bring them good luck to support the church.'

'And has it?'

'Not always, unfortunately.' Harbut grimaced. 'But I'm a big believer in tradition, and I've tried to continue in their footsteps. I'm a church warden at St. Joshua's, in fact, though I don't pull as much weight as I should these days. Pressure of work, and all that.'

Jack studied the photograph, but there was nothing particularly revealing about the stance of the two men. Vicar and church warden, sharing a positive moment. The sun shining low through the wych elms at the far end of the graveyard.

'Did you run in any of the races on the sports day?'

'I did, as a matter of fact. I didn't win, of course. Too many hours spent behind a desk. But I came a respectable third.'

'Who won?'

There was a momentary hesitation. 'A local man. Steve Watterson. Works with his father as a landscape gardener. The opposite of a desk job.'

'Grudge match, was it?'

'Not at all. I barely know the man.' Peter Harbut went to sit behind his desk, and again waved Jack towards one of the chairs for clients. 'Please, do sit down. How can I be of service?'

Jack sat directly opposite him and got out his notebook. 'You will have heard on the news that we found some, erm, remains recently at Tintagel.'

'I did hear something, yes. A dreadful business.'

'Well, I'm sorry to be the bearer of bad news.' Jack watched Harbut closely, though the man's expression had not changed. 'But we've since identified those remains as belonging to the Reverend Penhaligon.'

Harbut sat up, looking alarmed. 'Good God.'

'That's why I'm here. To ask you a few questions, try to get a clearer picture of his character and typical movements. As church warden, I imagine you must have seen more of the vicar than most of his parishioners.'

'I … I suppose so.' Harbut ran a hand through his blond thatch, leaving it more ruffled than ever.

'How well did the two of you get on?'

'Oh God.' The accountant seemed thoroughly discomposed now. 'Look, this has been a bit of a shock. Are these questions strictly necessary, detective sergeant? I mean, it's not like I had anything to do with his death.'

Jack raised his eyebrows and waited, notebook and pen in hand.

'How well did we get on?' Harbut repeated slowly. 'Not that well, to be honest. Rev Penhaligon is … ' He exhaled and corrected himself. '*Was* a prickly man. Hard to get along with. I shouldn't speak ill of the dead, but there it is. Though I believe he truly cared for St. Joshua's. The actual church building, that is. He was passionate about it. And the maintenance of the graveyard. The man dedicated himself to the place.'

'But you and he didn't get along? Why was that?'

'I told you, he wasn't an easy man to like. Bit of a short fuse, frankly. And some of his views were difficult to swallow. He could be infuriatingly old-fashioned at times.'

'Such as?'

Harbut hesitated, then said abruptly, 'His views on homosexuality, for a start. He called it an abomination.'

'In his sermons?'

'Oh no, he was very careful to tow the official line on Sundays. But privately … ' Harbut made a face. 'Full disclosure, detective sergeant. I'm a gay man. I got along just fine with the Rev until he discovered I had a male partner at home. Then he spent over a year trying to get rid of me in one way or another. Dirty tricks, bad mouthing me to the PPC – '

'PPC?'

'Parochial Parish Council. We oversee the the church and look after its various properties, and organise any associated activities.'

'Does that include the administration of church funds?'

'Of course.' Harbut stood up and paced the room, frowning. 'In the end, I suppose the Rev realised I wasn't going to let him bully me out of the position. Because he gave up.'

'But you were still angry about it. It caused bad blood between you.'

'I'm a practising Christian, detective sergeant. Forgiveness is key for us. But when it comes to my sexuality, that's another matter. I tried with Reverend Penhaligon, I really did. But I simply couldn't forgive and forget that kind of bigotry. So yes, it was still an issue between us.' Harbut sat down again, and gave him a direct look. 'But if you're thinking that's a motive for murder, you couldn't be further from the truth. I'm not just a Christian, I'm a pacifist. I could never harm anyone, it's not in my nature. So I had nothing to do with whatever happened to the Reverend.'

'And your partner? What's his name?'

Harbut stared. 'My ... partner? What's he got to do with this?'

'Nothing, hopefully. Just trying to get as full a picture as possible. We may need to speak to him too. What does he do for a living?'

The accountant looked stricken for a moment. Then he reached into his jacket pocket, took out his wallet, and removed a business card from it. This, he slid across the table towards Jack, his manner reluctant.

'You can reach him on that number. His name's Colm. He works in a bank in Bristol during the week. Only comes home at weekends.'

'Thank you.'

'He only met the Rev a few times though. Barely knew him to speak to. Colm's not a church goer. He's an atheist.'

Jack tucked the card into his notebook, and then made a few quick notes. He didn't entirely believe Peter Harbut's tale of the homophobe vicar. But it was plausible enough for now. Besides, Peter didn't strike him as the kind of hardened killer who could hack off a man's head – a difficult and messy task – and display it at Tintagel Castle. That took someone with a flair for the dramatic and macabre. Not to mention skill with sharp instruments. And while his partner Colm might have taken against the vicar for not accepting their relationship, as a banker he was unlikely to be moved to an act of savage butchery over it.

But there was still the small matter of thirty thousand pounds moving from the Reverend's bank account to his.

'Would you take a look at this for me?' He drew out the bank statement in its see-through evidence bag and passed it across the desk to Harbut. The accountant looked but did not touch, his eyes widening slightly as he saw what it was. 'You'll see the large amount halfway down the sheet. Thirty thousand pounds to a P. A Harbut.' He paused, watching the man's face. 'Is that you?'

Harbut swallowed, then nodded mutely.

'Can you explain the payment?'

'Erm, it was a … a loan.' Harbut pushed the bank statement back to him, definitely paler now, off-balance. 'A personal loan.'

Jack frowned. 'You're saying Reverend Penhaligon loaned you thirty thousand pounds?'

'That's right.'

'Even though he didn't like you? Didn't approve of your lifestyle?'

'Yes.'

'That doesn't seem quite believable.'

'It's true.'

'And what were the terms of this loan? Do you have paperwork on it?'

'We didn't see the need for paperwork.'

Jack was incredulous. 'But you hated him. And he hated you.'

'Hate is a very strong word.'

'Okay,' Jack said, frowning, 'let's say Penhaligon did agree to loan you thirty thousand pounds, without any kind of contract, which seems highly unlikely given the circumstances you've just explained to me. What exactly was the loan for?'

Harbut seemed to struggle for a moment, then closed his eyes briefly. When he opened them again, there was an air of pained resignation about him. 'The firm got into difficulties a couple of years back. There were some unfortunate discrepancies with our tax returns, which occasioned a large fine, and we've been bailing water ever since. I approached Charles – the Reverend Penhaligon – about the situation. He'd recently inherited a sizeable amount from some kind of distant relative, and I thought he might be willing to advance me a loan to get us through the next year.'

'And he was.'

'Yes.'

Jack studied him. 'Thirty thousand pounds is an extremely generous loan between private individuals. Especially given that you and the Reverend were not on the best of terms.'

'I suppose so, yes.'

'And the repayment terms?'

'It was a gentleman's agreement. Whenever I could repay, I would.'

Jack did not believe him.

'Was there any particular reason why he might have decided to loan you such a huge amount, Peter, without even a paper trail to protect him?'

The accountant flushed slightly. 'I ... I don't know what you mean, Detective Sergeant. We had our differences, yes, but there was also much that bound us together. We were both devout Christians, for instance.

And we both had the best interests of the church at heart.' He paused. 'St. Joshua's, especially.'

'And you won't mind us going through your files and computers to check that there was in fact no paperwork on this loan?'

'Oh no, feel free to look about.' Harbut looked almost relieved. 'I have nothing to hide. I mean, not since you already know about the loan. I should have told you about the money upfront. But I thought it would make me look guilty.'

'Yes,' Jack said drily.

Peter Harbut had known something about the Reverend Penhaligon, he decided. Something uncomfortable or embarrassing, that the vicar probably hadn't wanted his parishioners to discover. Bad enough, perhaps, that the church itself might have suffered by its disclosure.

Hence the extraordinary loan, on even more extraordinary terms.

Hush money.

But what had Penhaligon been trying so desperately to hide? With most vicars, the obvious leap would be towards some kind of sexual misdemeanour or perversion. That was what usually got parishioners' knickers in a twist. The other typical alternative was a drinking problem. But in this case, there could be a twist of a more complicated kind.

He thought of what they'd found in the Reverend's private study. Those bizarre items more readily associated with black magic than a Church of England vicar. Had that been Charles Penhaligon's dirty secret? That he'd been up to his neck in Satanic rituals rather than drinking the communion wine or seducing his flock? While all that blether about sinful homosexuals and his daughter's obsession with astrology had been an elaborate smokescreen …

But all this still didn't give him either a suspect or a strong motive for murder. If there had been a possible demand for the return of his money, that would have provided both.

But, without any kind of paperwork for proof, Charles Penhaligon must have known he couldn't force Peter Harbut to repay that loan. No court in the land would have enforced such a repayment without a contract of some kind between the two parties. It would have been seen as a 'gift', and Peter would have walked away from it. Besides which, if the loan had been made originally in order to hush up some guilty secret, there was no way the vicar would have taken Peter to court over non-repayment.

'So, can you think of anyone who might have wanted to harm him?' he asked, finishing his notes.

'Of course I can't. The man was a vicar, after all.' Harbut paused, then frowned. 'Though, having said that … There was an incident recently with a woman parishioner. Quite an ugly incident, in fact.'

'Go on.'

Harbut looked thoughtful. 'I'm not sure of the details. But the rumour was that a woman had made a complaint against him to the church.'

'Against Reverend Penhaligon?'

'That's right.'

'What kind of complaint?'

'Sexual assault. I heard on the grapevine that the Rev had touched her up. Or she'd claimed he did. I don't know if there was anything in it.'

'Did she report him to the police?'

'I have no idea, I'm afraid. But I doubt it.' Harbut shrugged. 'It was one of those six day wonders. The bishop swooped on us, the woman had her say, the Rev had his, and then the whole thing was hushed up.'

Jack stared. 'But if she was assaulted – '

'Look, detective, you don't understand.' Harbut leant forward, his expression earnest. 'The church has to protect itself against things like this. We have enough problems keeping believers as it is. And this woman, she has … That is, she seems to have serious mental health issues.'

'Could you be more specific?'

'She makes things up. Crazy things, things that couldn't possibly be true.' He pulled a wry face. 'Plus, she had a major thing for the Rev at the time. Everybody knew.'

'You mean a sexual thing?'

Harbut nodded. 'She used to hang about after Sunday communion just to get him alone. And she got drunk in the churchyard a few times and shouted at people like a mad woman. I had to move her on myself more than once. So when she claimed that he'd touched her – '

'You didn't believe her.' Jack tried not to let his anger show. 'How long ago was this alleged assault?'

'I don't know, maybe six or seven months ago?'

'And the woman's name?'

'Fifi Maggs, with a double g.' Harbut watched Jack write it down in his notebook. 'She's homeless; lives in a ramshackle old tent down by the river, in the field below the church. We've often tried to get her to leave, but … Well, the Rev always stopped us.'

'Even after the alleged assault?'

'Oh yes. The field where she pitches her tent is church property, you see, and the Rev had a thing about charity. *There but for the grace of God go I*, you know?'

Jack nodded.

This Fifi Maggs sounded like someone he needed to contact, he decided, and as soon as possible. Probably a job he could hand to Ronny while he checked through the items they'd taken from the vicar's attic study.

'The woman's a complete oddball. You should definitely question her.' Harbut blinked, perhaps realising the inference of what he'd said, and swiftly backtracked. 'I'm not saying she's done anything wrong, of course. But if anyone knows who's been coming and going at the vicarage recently, it'll be Fifi.'

Jack hesitated, then threw out a line to see what he might catch. 'Really? What about Stella Penhaligon, though? Wouldn't she know more about her father's movements?'

'The vicar's daughter?'

'Do you know her?'

'Not particularly. I mean, I know her to speak to. But Stella hasn't been around the place much for a good few years. There was a falling out between her and the Rev, and she moved out.'

So she hadn't been lying about that, Jack thought.

His mobile rang, and he glanced at the screen.

Caller Unknown.

'Well, you've been very helpful,' Jack said, and placed a business card on the accountant's desk. 'Contact me if you think of anything else.'

'Of course.'

'If you'll excuse me, I have to answer this call.'

'Hello? DS Church speaking.'

Jack stepped out of the entrance door into the glow of late afternoon sunlight, the mobile to his ear, and narrowly avoided collision with a woman pushing a buggy. He crossed the road, heading back to the car park where he'd left his car.

'It's Stella Penhaligon.' The vicar's daughter sounded on edge, breathless. 'You asked me to call if … if I needed to speak to you about anything. Are you free to talk?'

'I have a few minutes, yes.'

'You remember I told you that I'm an astrologer?'

'How could I forget?'

'Well, I know you told me to leave everything to the police, but … when I got back home earlier, I drew up a horary chart.'

'I beg your pardon?'

'Horary. It's a special branch of astrology used for answering specific questions and also for locating missing objects.'

'Missing objects,' Jack repeated, shaking his head. He unlocked his car and got inside. 'Why do I have a bad feeling about where this is headed?'

'Please don't make fun of this, Detective Sergeant Church.'

'Sorry. I'm listening.'

'Thank you.' She took a deep breath. 'I drew up a horary chart and studied it. And I think I know where to find the rest of … my father's body.'

'From a birth chart?'

'A horary chart. There's a big difference.'

'Okay.' Jack closed his eyes briefly, willing himself to be patient. 'And where exactly do you think his body is, Miss Penhaligon?'

'St. Nectan's Glen.'

Jack opened his eyes again, trying not to rush his response to that. She obviously believed in this astrological nonsense.

But the suggestion was ludicrous.

St. Nectan's Glen was a popular tourist spot on the north coast of his patch. It had a wooded area with an impressive waterfall, and a pool at the bottom of the glen where New Age types often left 'offerings' to whatever god or spirit they believed in, and sometimes memorials to loved ones. Candles, flowers, photos in plastic, that kind of thing. The worst they'd ever found down there were the remnants of drug use, plus occasional illegal over-night camping. People walked there most days in all seasons, though. Hardly the kind of place where you'd dump a body.

Besides, the path down to the bottom of the glen was narrow and winding, and frequently muddy after poor weather. Manoeuvring it with a headless corpse would be a difficult task even for the most ruthless or well-prepared killer. Not to mention messy.

Still, he had to remember that the woman was probably still in shock. And shock made people say and do strange things.

Gently does it, he told himself.

'So, how exactly did you work all that out from an astrological chart?' He opened his eyes and watched traffic on the High Street moving slowly. It was still early in the season, but visitors were already beginning to return to Cornwall. Which meant increased numbers of cars on the roads. 'Or shouldn't I ask?'

'It's quite a complex thing, horary. I can't explain properly without showing you the chart.'

'Right.'

'Though I could send it to your phone.' She paused. 'The chart image, I mean. Then I could talk you through it.'

'Erm, that won't be necessary.'

Jack wondered if the Reverend's daughter was actually crazy, or whether she had inside information about her father's death and was couching it as an 'astrological insight' in order to avoid suspicion.

Either way, he needed to humour her.

'So,' he continued carefully, 'if I were to head over there right now, whereabouts in St. Nectan's Glen should I be looking?'

'I'm not sure.'

'I see.'

'That is, it could be somewhere along the coastal path too, near the glen, but not actually inside it. It's not an exact science.'

'That's quite an extensive area for a search, Miss Penhaligon. Could you try to be a little more specific? To save police time.'

Stella didn't answer for a moment, then said slowly, as though trying not to reveal too much, 'Somewhere ... hidden.'

'That does seem likely.' His mouth twitched, but somehow he managed to keep the laughter out of his voice. 'Otherwise I think we would have had multiple reports of a body by now, Miss Penhaligon. It's quite popular with ramblers and dog walkers, St. Nectan's Glen.'

'Yes, that's what I thought too,' she said earnestly. 'So, obviously, it must be somewhere out of sight. But there could be a tree involved too.'

'A tree.'

'Or several trees. That part ... I'm not really clear about. But it's somewhere dark and low down, and probably near water too.'

'Well, thank you for that.' Jack turned on his ignition, abruptly losing interest in this bizarre conversation.

There could be a tree involved. Or several trees. The woman was certifiable. 'Look, I tell you what, I'll send someone over to the glen to take a look around. But it probably won't be today, I'm afraid.'

'Detective – '

'We're stretched thin as it is. This isn't the Met, it's the South-West. I have to prioritise resources. And it would be dark by the time I could get a proper search team organised.'

'But the chart says … '

'I'm sorry to cut you off, Miss Penhaligon. I'm needed urgently back at the station. Thank you for the information. We'll be in touch.' He rang off and shook his head in disbelief. 'Astrology. *A tree*. Whatever next? She must be bloody crackers.'

CHAPTER ELEVEN

Stella put down the phone handset, staring blankly at nothing.

'Well?' Nick asked impatiently.

'He didn't believe me. He said … He said this wasn't the Met, and that his resources are stretched thin.'

'So he's not sending anyone there?'

'Not today.'

'Tomorrow, then?'

'He didn't actually say when.' Stella closed her eyes, feeling light-headed. Perhaps the shock of the past twenty-four hours was finally catching up with her. 'In fact, I'm not sure that DS Church is going to bother looking in St. Nectan's Glen at all.'

'Seriously? But why not?'

'Isn't it obvious, Nick? The man thinks I'm crazy.' Stella gestured helplessly to the horary chart, still pulled up on her computer screen. 'And can you blame him? To most people, astrology isn't real. It's ... a joke to them, a game, something on the level of a Ouija board or tarot readings from a fairground booth.'

'I guess so.'

'It's certainly not a science, or a way of living in the real world.' Stella spotted his look of hesitation. 'And yes, I know you don't believe in astrology one hundred percent either. Or even fifty percent.' Her smile was weary. 'There's no need to pretend.'

'I just want to be supportive.'

'And you are.'

'I'm your friend, Stella. We're house mates. Yeah, maybe I don't fully believe in all that astrology ... stuff. But I believe that you believe it, and hey, you've had a rough time lately. Your dad getting murdered by some bloody maniac. And then, having to identify his ...' To her relief, Nick dropped that gruesome sentence without finishing it. 'I mean, God, I can't even imagine how that would feel.'

'Probably better not to try.'

'And you've still got a sense of humour about it. I love that about you. It's what makes you special.'

'Oh, is that what it is?'

'Look, Stella …' Nick put a hand on her shoulder, meeting her gaze. 'I'm here for you. What do you want to do?'

'You know what I want to do.'

'Does it involve going for a drink with me at the Cornishman tonight? Or maybe to a film at the Rebel Cinema? They do great popcorn.'

'Sorry.'

'That's okay, maybe another time.' Nick looked thoughtfully at the chart on the computer screen. 'You want to head over to the glen and look for your dad yourself, don't you?'

'I've got to,' she said simply. 'It's obvious the police aren't going to. Which only leaves me. What would you do, if it was your dad?'

'Exactly the same, I guess.' Nick stretched and yawned behind his hand, fatigue in his face, and then shook himself like a dog coming out of water. 'Okay, I'm going with you to the glen. Give me five minutes. I need to change into some proper walking boots and grab a sandwich to eat on the way. I'm starving!'

'I don't need you to come along,' she said hurriedly, reaching for her coat. 'Honestly, I … I don't want company.'

She didn't exactly relish the thought of hunting alone for her father's remains, especially as it would be early evening soon and the light would begin to fail in a few hours. But the last thing she needed was to encourage Nick to think she was interested in him romantically. They were friends, that was all. And she didn't entirely trust him not to understand that.

'Of course you don't. Nothing spooky about any of this. You'll be fine.'

'Nick, you've just come back from work, for God's sake.' She had carefully decided not to address his sarcasm. 'I can't drag you all the way down St. Nectan's Glen on a wild goose chase.'

'Hey, what are housemates for?' Nick turned in the doorway to grin back at her. 'Besides, you believe in all this astrology shit. So it can't be a wild goose chase, can it?'

The sun was worryingly low on the western horizon by the time she and Nick parked in the small free car park above St. Nectan's Glen and began to make their way towards the site. That involved a quick trudge uphill first, past an allegedly holy well opposite the small fifteenth century church of St. Piran, and its equally ancient former monastery, semi-fortified walls sagging in places and overgrown. The track opened up beyond the houses, overlooking fields, cliffs and the soft blue of the Atlantic, lying peaceful today.

Shortly after the last property along the single-track lane, they entered St. Nectan's Glen itself, and took the rocky, wooded track down towards the river in the valley bottom.

Stella studied the sky through the high green canopy of leaves, uneasy now. How long before the light failed?

Her pressing sense of urgency would make it unbearable for them to wait until tomorrow to search the glen, yet she knew it would be pointless once dusk had fallen.

'Thank you for coming with me,' she said again.

'Least I could do.' Nick shot her a strained smile. 'Though if we do find something, it's not likely to be pleasant. You realise that?'

'Of course.'

'But you're still determined to look.'

'I know it probably seems strange to you – '

'Just a tad.'

'But I won't be able to sleep tonight without having tried to find him,' Stella said, turning her head from side to side as they descended the mud track, peering through gigantic overgrown rhododendron bushes and between creeper-hung trees. She wasn't exactly sure what she was looking for. But she had a suspicion she would know it when she saw it. 'I just have this awful feeling that I'm right to look here.'

A little way around the next bend, they passed an old man and his dog, coming up slowly from the glen. The old man nodded at them, the dog paused to frolic about them briefly, his shaggy flanks and paws still wet from a swimming expedition, and then they were alone again in the stillness of the early evening.

Beside the river in the valley bottom was a grove of rhododendrons, huge and glossy-leaved. On the other side were beeches, some tall and majestic, others leaning at a precarious angle, most covered in moss and ivy creepers.

Along the way, passers-by had tied coloured ribbons to some of the overhanging branches. Some of the ribbons were old and frayed at the ends. Others looked brand-new, their colours still fresh.

Votive offerings, she thought, glancing up at them.

Stella slowed her steps before they reached the river, suddenly alert to something different. The track was muddier there than elsewhere, a clump of wild plants oddly crushed in one spot before the mossy bank. Beyond the bank, she could see brambles parted on either side of a flattened patch, with mud churned up, the damage extending beyond the track for quite a way into the trees …

'Hold on,' Stella said, grabbing at Nick's arm as he would have passed her. 'Wait a minute. Look at that.'

He turned back, frowning. 'What are we looking at?'

'The undergrowth past the bank … It's all trodden down.' She prodded one of the muddied, crumpled plants with the toe of her boot. 'And something's been dragged through here. Something heavy.'

'If you say so.'

'The plants have been crushed further in too. Almost like a mini-track.' She took a step off the path, and glanced back at him. 'This is the place. I feel it. Look, there's water.' She indicated the rushing river ahead. 'And we're fairly low down now.'

'I thought you said it had to be somewhere holy. Or with offerings, or something. Like the waterfall? That's further on.'

'And what are those?' She pointed to the ribbons tied to branches on either side of the track. 'Or those.' Further along the track, a fallen tree trunk, closely studded with embedded coins, had been displayed for tourists. She remembered trying to count them once on a previous visit, and being astonished at how many hundreds of coins had been pressed into the decaying wood. 'This is it, Nick.'

'But the waterfall is the most holy place in the glen, isn't it?'

'Horary charts can be approximate. I often have to feel my way sideways into an interpretation. The chart led me to St. Nectan's Glen, that's all I can be sure of. Somewhere dimly lit, low down, with water, a place of ritual. But this … ' She stared into the deepening woodland. 'My instincts tell me to go this way.'

Nick shrugged. 'If your instincts think it's worth tramping through the mud to look for a body, who am I to argue with them?'

'Don't be such a wimp.' She climbed the mossy bank that ran along the track, and plunged over it into woodland. 'Come on, before it gets dark.'

They followed the trail of flattened undergrowth and broken green shoots for several minutes, wandering further and further from the path. Someone had definitely come through here recently, she thought, and with a heavy or unwieldy load. Though the marks were so subtle, she had to stop occasionally and take a fresh bearing.

'It could have been a forester,' Nick pointed out, reasonably. 'Someone looking after the glen, coppicing maybe, keeping down growth.'

'Maybe.'

Stella kept going, regardless. Some instinct was driving her, and though she wasn't sure she liked the feeling, there was no ignoring it.

The trail led them through a cluster of younger birch trees, and into a sudden dip where an ancient beech rose out of leaf detritus like a god.

The beech's thick, lichened trunk was dark with old stains, clumps of ivy clinging and creeping. Something had badly damaged the trunk years ago, leaving a cleft in the wood. Just below the ugly, ribbed cleft, something dull and discoloured, perhaps a thick rope, had been wrapped about the trunk and tied in a kind of rough, bulbous bow.

The earth at the base of the tree had been disturbed. And recently too. She could see several bulging lumps under the soil, covered up in leaves and twigs, as though someone had tried inadequately to conceal the disturbance.

Stella stopped, swallowing.

Even without the odd heaps of soil around and between the old tree's roots, the grim smell would have been enough to tell her this was the place.

'Jesus Christ Almighty.'

'I know.'

But Nick was not looking at the lumpy mess of leaves under the beech. 'Stella, don't … don't go any closer.' He fumbled a mobile out of his coat pocket, his hands shaking. 'Shit, I'd better call the police. What … What's that detective's number?'

'Not yet, we need to be sure.'

He stared at her, a look of abject horror in his face, then pointed to the beech trunk. 'But … *that*,' was all he managed to say, his voice hoarse.

Stella followed his gaze, and with a sick dread realised what he meant.

'Oh my God.'

The strange, bulbous rope knotted about the discoloured trunk …

It was no rope, she could see that now, but an uncoiled length of smooth intestines. Human intestines, stinking and jewelled with flies in the warmth of the spring evening.

She clamped a hand to her mouth.

'Come away!' Nick urged her. 'You shouldn't look.'

'No ... I need to ... '

Half-maddened by the thought of what had been done to her father's body, the vile, sacrilegious indignity of his death, Stella dropped to her knees before the largest lump and began to scoop away camouflaging leaves and twigs, then earth in great soggy clumps, her hands shaking.

'Stella, for Christ's sake ... !'

But she ignored him, suddenly deaf to his entreaties, driven by a mindless frenzy she couldn't control or understand. All she knew was that it was impossible for her to stop digging between the roots of the old beech, as though she'd been possessed in some dreadful way, perhaps by her own guilt, or by something beyond human comprehension.

Behind her, she was vaguely aware of Nick on the phone, speaking to someone in a low, urgent voice.

The police?

Her fingernails blackened with soil, Stella stopped, jerking her hands away in horror. For a moment, it was hard to breathe.

She had hit flesh.

Dirty, ash-white flesh streaked with mud.

A man's torso.

The loose, baggy skin was marked with dark red, deep-etched symbols that looked like they'd been cut into the flesh with a knife.

With one sickened glance, she recognised an inverted cross inside a pentagram, and beneath it, one set of double wave squiggles like the sigil for the air sign Aquarius.

But it was only a torso in the shallow pit she'd dug out.

Nothing more.

She stared at the other lumpy heaps around the tree, all poorly camouflaged with leaf mess like this one, and fell back gasping and retching.

'Dad,' she moaned. 'Dad …'

CHAPTER TWELVE

Stella Penhaligon was still waiting at the top of the glen when Jack, having left the forensics team doing their work, climbed back up the dark wooded path from St. Nectan's Glen, checking his way with a torch.

The vicar's daughter looked pale and wide-eyed with shock, wrapped in a silver thermal blanket and perched on the back steps of the waiting ambulance. The single-track road was not exactly ideal for emergency vehicle access, but they had got permission to park on several drives of adjacent properties. Ronny had conducted a quick door-to-door, but nobody had heard or seen anything suspicious, of course. Just the usual steady stream of tourists and dog walkers going up and down the glen path for the past week.

Blue police lights strafed the dusk about her, bouncing off drystone walls and hedgerows in the narrow country lane.

Who the hell was she?

What was she?

He had been so sure at the outset that Stella Penhaligon was harmless. An eccentric, yes. But not a suspect. Now, he couldn't look at the woman without harbouring the gravest suspicions about her motives and character.

How the hell had she known where to find her father's remains?

She had asked him on the phone earlier to look here, claiming that an astrological chart had sent her to St. Nectan's Glen.

He had not believed her, and he was still not convinced. Who would dump a body here, in a remote beauty spot on the raggedy edge of the Cornish north coast? And it wasn't exactly a small site, a good mile's walk from the car park on the main coast road to the waterfall at the base of the glen. Yet from what her friend had told Ronny in his initial statement, Stella Penhaligon had gone to the right tree almost unerringly.

Astrology.

The 'stars' had told her where to look, she'd told the first police on the scene following her 999 call. As though she expected them to believe that.

She'd mentioned a tree on the phone earlier.

Jack had laughed.

He wasn't laughing now. Not after seeing – and smelling – the bloodied tribute wrapped about the beech trunk like a gory ribbon. Human intestines, the SOCO had told him, with an air of certainty and not a little disgust.

Her father's innards.

'How are you bearing up, Miss Penhaligon?' he asked her, deciding to hide his suspicions for now. He jiggled loose change in his pocket, his brain working overtime. 'That must have been quite a shock.'

'I'm okay.' Her voice was thin though, and she looked exhausted. 'Was it … Is it definitely him?'

'We won't know for a few days yet. Forensics can take a while.'

'It does seem likely though.'

He could not deny that, meeting her questioning look with a grimace. North Cornwall was hardly knee-deep in headless corpses. Especially ones marked with symbols that linked back to the kind of black magic shit they'd found in the Reverend's secret study.

But he couldn't confirm it either. Not unless he wanted DI Martin on his back. This woman was a suspect now. She had found the victim's remains too easily.

Astrology. There was no way, he thought grimly.

'I'm afraid I can't speculate at this stage.' He paused, seeing some flicker in her face. Disappointment? Frustration? 'Not officially.'

'But?'

He met her eyes, trying to read guilt or guile in them, and finding nothing there but a stark despair.

'But it does seem likely,' he agreed reluctantly.

'Someone cut him up. Who would do that? It's so sick. What kind of person … ' Stella groaned. 'That was only his torso I found. So the rest of him … Those other mounds … ' She swallowed convulsively. 'They chopped him into bits, didn't they?'

'*They?*'

'Whoever did this, I mean.'

He searched her face intently. 'And you still have no idea who that is? The murderer?'

'I told you everything I knew.'

Jack frowned. 'You don't mind talking about this? Don't get me wrong but you seem pretty calm, considering what you've just seen down there.'

'I'm not calm,' she said flatly.

'You should go home.'

'Nick brought me in his car.' She looked about distractedly. 'Where … Where is he? I think he's gone.'

'I suggested your friend should leave once he'd given a statement to my constable. Look, it's not a problem. I'll get an officer to drive you home.'

'Thank you.'

She stood up, handing the silver blanket back to the paramedic with a few murmured words of thanks. Then they walked across to where Ronny's car was parked, nestled onto someone's drive, blue lights flashing.

It was clear she was still in shock. But shock over the discovery of her father's remains, or the shock of guilt over what she herself had done?

He knew from experience that these two responses could look eerily similar in the early stages after the report of a crime, and before extensive questioning began to reveal flaws and gaps in a suspect's story. For now though, he decided to assume innocence. Not least because it might make her more likely to slip up …

'Is Nick your boyfriend?'

'Housemate.' She shivered. 'I told you before, I live in a shared house. Nick didn't want me to come out here alone, that's all. He can be very … chivalrous at times.'

Jack nodded, not sure whether to believe her. Nick Farley. He had spoken to the man briefly before leaving him with Ronny in order to investigate the crime scene. Fair-haired, good-looking, about thirty years old, and clearly muscular. He worked as a carer in one of the many residential homes in this part of Cornwall. Strong, in other words, and used to a wide cross-section of unsavoury tasks, including contact with the recently deceased.

They, she had said. *They chopped him into bits, didn't they?*

Had 'they' been a guilty slip of a murderer's tongue, or an innocent use of plural for singular?

Nick can be very chivalrous at times.

So chivalrous that he came out in the evening with her to a remote beauty spot in order to hunt for her dead father's remains? Men only tended to be *that* chivalrous when they were sexually involved with a woman, in his experience. Or hoped to be.

Nick Farley was fit and active-looking. He could have carried those body parts down the glen for her, off the path into the undergrowth, and then buried them according to her instructions under the huge beech. Or helped her bury them. He might even have wrapped the intestines about the tree trunk for her.

A messy job though, as Ronny had quickly pointed out. And both of them had appeared clean. Except for Stella Penhaligon's hands and knees, of course, soiled by her impromptu grave-digging. Though the two of them might have buried those remains at any time over the past few days, gone home and cleaned up, carefully disposing of anything that might incriminate them, and then returned today in order to stage their discovery.

Nick had appeared protective towards her, Ronny had said. Almost proprietorial. Why, if the man wasn't her boyfriend?

And they had come out here together.

'Neither of you should have come here today,' he said, stopping beside Ronny's police car. The detective constable was nowhere to be seen. Perhaps he had gone back down into the glen. 'I told you on the phone that I would send someone to investigate.'

'But when?' Her gaze flicked angrily to his face, her voice laced with abrupt accusation. 'I'm not stupid, DS Church. I knew you didn't believe me. That you don't believe in astrology.'

'Most people don't believe in astrology.'

She shrugged that off, looking away. 'Maybe I didn't get on with him, but he was still my father, for God's sake. I had to do something.'

'What you did, Miss Penhaligon, was interfere with a crime scene. Which is an arrestable offence.'

'So arrest me!'

Jack bit back his temper. This approach was counter-productive. Baiting her. 'Of course I don't want to arrest you. But you must admit, it does look a little suspicious.'

'I wondered how long it would take the police to accuse me of having something to do with that ... that *depravity*.' She glared at him. 'Nick was right. Before you lot finally turned up, he warned me – '

She stopped dead.

'Yes?' Jack folded his arms, waiting. 'What did Nick say?'

'He said you wouldn't believe that an astrological chart helped me find my father. That I'd do better telling you I'm psychic.'

'Are you?'

'Of course not.' She sounded contemptuous. 'And being psychic ... At best, it's a difficult burden to carry, and at worst a complete scam. It's certainly got nothing to do with astrology. What I do is a science. A genuine discipline. People have been practising astrology successfully for millennia, and for good reason.'

'Because it makes money?'

'Because it works,' she almost spat at him. 'Not that I would expect you to understand something as simple as that, DS Church. To you, I'm a freak. Or a fraud.'

He said nothing, studying her white, tormented face. *To you, I'm a freak. Or a fraud.* That was actually pretty much his exact position. Perhaps her rejection of psychic powers had been premature.

'I want to go home now, if you've finished with this interrogation.' Stella tugged her jacket closer about herself, her voice uneven. 'It's cold, and I can't think what else to tell you, except that I ... I didn't do it.'

Her voice had risen angrily, and several other officers, coming up the track from the glen, were looking their way in surprise. He saw Ronny among them, and lifted a hand to call him over.

'You're free to go, Miss Penhaligon. Though I expect we'll need to talk to you again. Probably once the forensics reports is back.'

Once Ronny had helped Stella into the car, and driven away with her into the thickening dark, Jack made his way back down the wooded path into the glen, lighting his way with a torch.

Forensics had erected a white tent and portable high-intensity lights about the site, several people milling about in plastic-covered shoes, the photographer hard at work. The team had only just finished a fingertip search at Tintagel Castle before the light failed this evening. Now they were here instead, digging up body parts. He could see fatigue on some of the faces. But at least nobody was complaining.

'Hello again,' he told the SOCO.

'No rest for the wicked, eh?' Cameron gave him a faint grin, pulling on a fresh pair of latex gloves. 'I'd laid bets we wouldn't get to reunite head and trunk for some weeks. That'll teach me not to be so sceptical.'

'So, what have we got?'

'At a rough estimate, I'd say most of the missing body parts are here.' Cameron was looking almost pleased by this result, macabre soul that he was. 'The other burial mounds around the tree contain legs, arms, hands, feet. I've left most of them in situ for now, until we can complete a proper forensic examination of the site.'

'Jesus.'

'There was only the most rudimentary attempt to hide them. Maybe a few inches of soil and leaves on top of each find. The shallowest of graves.'

Jack frowned, stooping to examine the largest find so far. The torso, mangled and marked with strange symbols. 'I wonder why?'

'Someone clearly wanted the site to be found, despite choosing a spot away from the main path. The body parts were buried, yes. Including the penis, which had been severed.'

'Jesus.'

'But the intestines wrapped about the trunk …' Cameron gave him another lopsided grin. 'Dramatic, to say the least. And very public. No attempt at concealment there.'

'You think whoever did this wanted it to be found easily?'

'I'm just telling you what I've found. In my opinion, if you want it – '

'I do, as it happens.'

'I think the intestines were hung up almost like a grave marker.' Cameron glanced up at them, still hanging about the broad girth of the beech, not to be removed until forensics had finished a fingertip search of the scene. 'Like a personalised headstone. Or an invitation to the observer.'

'What, *dig here*?'

'Something like that, perhaps. Or a warning, perhaps.'

'A warning?' Jack frowned, struck by that idea for some reason. 'Against what?'

Cameron shrugged. 'If I knew that, I'd be the detective sergeant, and you'd be the one wearing latex gloves and plastic shoes.'

They stood aside as the photographer entered the narrow space of the tent, nodding to them without speaking. Jack watched silently as she took a few more flash-lit shots of the uncovered male torso, still protruding from the soil where Stella had brushed away the earth, and then moved on to photograph the intestines and other burial mounds with their gruesome contents.

'Thanks, Joan,' Cameron said cheerily when she'd finished.

Jack crouched to study the pagan symbols cut deep into the white flesh. The pentagram hardly needed any comment. Black magic, for sure.

Stella Penhaligon had been wearing a silver pentagram around her neck at their first meeting. And though she had denied being psychic, with every evidence of loathing, there was something very witchy about her. The black clothing, the astrological connection …

'Just out of interest,' Jack asked, 'what do you make of these markings? Made with a knife?'

'I'll get a full report to you as soon as possible. But off the top of my head, this definitely looks ritual to me. A cult killing.'

'And this?'

Jack pointed carefully, without making contact with the skin, to the two wavy lines carved out beneath the five-pointed shape.

'I'd say that's probably some kind of … astrological symbol?' Cameron shrugged. 'At a guess.'

CHAPTER THIRTEEN

'Can you confirm your whereabouts last Sunday, Miss Penhaligon?'

A week ago today, she thought.

It felt more like a lifetime, so much had happened between then and now. Most of it in the last turbulent forty-eight hours.

Stella placed her hands flat on the desk between them and looked into the detective's eyes. DS Church wasn't a bad-looking man, she thought. Under other circumstances, she might even have found him attractive. But right now he seemed like the most hateful person she knew.

How could he put her through this ordeal, knowing what she had already suffered this week?

She was trying hard to keep it together. But her heart was thumping and there was a clamminess to her palms that had nothing to do with attraction and everything to do with fear.

The police thought she must have been involved in her father's murder. Because of astrology. Because of the horary chart she'd drawn up to find his remains. Because she was too good at her job.

The irony did not escape her.

'I was at home,' she said, thinking back to that day with difficulty. 'It was an ordinary Sunday. Nothing much happening. I slept late. Went for a pub lunch with Julie and Claire – '

'The two teachers you live with?'

'That's right.'

DS Church nodded, watching her intently. 'Which pub?'

'The Cornishman.'

'Do you think they'll remember you?'

'I paid my share with a credit card. That proof enough?'

'Not really. Someone else could have used your card. You could have given your PIN to your friends.'

She sat back, staring at him. 'For God's sake … '

'And after lunch?'

'We went for a walk along the river. Then back to the house with the others. They were redecorating the living room that afternoon. And I had work to do.'

'What kind of work?'

'The astrological type, of course. A birth chart for a new client.' She frowned, struggling to remember her exact movements that day. 'I'd been working on it for a couple of weeks, and was just finishing up.'

'Do birth charts always take that long?'

'Pretty much. Though it depends on how complicated they are. Not all birth charts are the same.'

'Clearly,' he said drily, 'or you'd be out of a job.'

She wondered what star sign he was, and was tempted to ask for the detective's birth data. Smack him out of this light, mocking tone by showing how much she could tell about his life, his past, his character, all with a few simple clicks of a mouse. But there was no point alienating him.

'Then I had supper, watched some telly with Nick – '

'Who isn't your boyfriend.'

'That's right.'

The look in his eyes told her he still didn't believe her. 'And then?'

'I expect I had a quick bath and went to bed.'

'Nothing else.'

She shook her head, then caught herself up short. 'Apart from … ' She hesitated, frowning.

'Yes?'

'Apart from the message Dad sent me. I think that was on Sunday.' She took out her phone and unlocked it. 'Yes. Sunday.'

'We'll need your phone.' He held out a hand. 'Is it password-protected?'

Reluctantly, she handed it over and showed him the pattern code that unlocked it. He made a note and slipped the phone into an evidence bag.

'So, does all this mean I'm a suspect?'

'Not at all, Miss Penhaligon.' He looked across the desk at her steadily. 'This interview is about eliminating you from our enquiries.'

'I'm free to go, then?'

'Not quite.'

DS Church opened the folder in front of him and began methodically removing and sorting through a series of photocopied sheets.

She spotted letters, bank statements, photos of items from her father's private study, the markings she'd seen on her father's grim torso, among others. There were photographs of the vicarage grounds too, and even the meadow below it, including a long-distance shot of what looked like Fifi Maggs standing beside her tent by the river, turned away from the camera.

It looked like the police had been investigating every area of her father's life in their search for clues about his death.

These, the detective arranged carefully in front of her. 'First, Miss Penhaligon, I'd like to talk to you about some of these. Then, I'd like to go over your movements for the rest of the week. Finally, I'll need the names of your clients and anyone else you've spent time with recently.'

'My clients?' She glared at him. 'But that's confidential information. You can't make me divulge that.'

His smile chilled her.

For the first time since they'd brought her in for this unexpected second interview, she felt in real danger.

'Actually,' he told her softly, 'in a murder enquiry, I can. And I'll be keeping you here until I'm satisfied that you've told me everything.'

'In that case,' Stella said, 'I've changed my mind. I'd like a lawyer to be present.'

'Of course.' Jack Church sat back, the intensity of his gaze making her uncomfortable. 'I can arrange that.'

The duty lawyer took over an hour to arrive at the station. He turned out to be a sweating, pudgy man with serious bad breath and an ill-fitting suit. But he knew his stuff, and after fifteen minutes had Stella out of the place and free to return home.

'Next time they bring you in,' he told her in the car park, 'give me a call.' The lawyer handed over his business card, Marcus Escutcheon written across it in flowing black script. 'I'll sit in on any future interviews, make sure you get treated properly.'

'But I didn't do anything wrong. I had nothing to do with my father's death. I don't understand why the police think I did.'

'They're just fishing for a lead. Don't worry about it. They have no evidence and no witnesses, and therefore no legal reason to hold you for questioning.'

'I feel awful,' Stella said. 'I feel … exhausted.'

'I'm not surprised, after what you've been through lately. Go home, put your feet up.' He shook her hand. 'And call my office if you need any advice.'

'Thank you.'

She got back into her car and sat there for several minutes, staring blankly at the red brick wall of the police station.

Then she backed out slowly and turned her car in the direction of the north coast and Pethporro.

Putting her feet up sounded like good advice, but she wasn't going home. Not yet. There was something she needed to do first.

CHAPTER FOURTEEN

Stella parked in the same place as last time and got out, looking around. The road was deserted, a typical Sunday afternoon vibe to the place. The churchyard stood quiet and empty in the spring sunshine, except for a burly, bald-headed man in T-shirt and shorts cutting the grass between headstones. There had been no communion service this morning, apparently, but a notice on the board in the church porch announced a vigil and memorial service for the Reverend Penhaligon to be held the following weekend.

Yesterday, Stella had been consulted about the memorial service by the bishop, whose phone call had surprised her.

'Such a terrible loss,' the bishop had said in his mild way, and then asked if she would like to say something at the memorial service.

Stella had agreed, though with misgiving. It was still not clear what her father had been involved in. But until she knew for certain, it was more respectful to assume the best and not mention any of the other stuff.

Today, there was police tape across the vicarage gate, along with a POLICE DO NOT ENTER sign on the front door.

Stella studied the familiar house in silence, thinking of everything that had happened, and then walked past the house, taking the grassy path that led to the river meadow.

Fifi Maggs was a shadowy figure on the edge of the woodlands that bordered the meadow, bending to gather sticks for her fire.

Stella stopped beside her ancient, heavily patched tent, and wondered again where Fifi was from originally. Not that it mattered much. She had been camping in Church Meadow for years, a shambolic figure cooking over her little fire, occasionally begging for food and clothing at the church or even in Pethporro, when she could bring herself to walk that far.

After so long, she felt like part of the landscape.

Fifi must have heard her crossing the meadow because she suddenly straightened, turning to peer in

Stella's direction. 'Who … Who's that?' There was a note of panic in her hoarse voice as she clutched the bundle of dry wood to her chest. 'Who are you? Go on, get away from my things.'

'It's only me, Fifi. Stella Penhaligon. Don't you recognise me?'

Fifi came stumbling back towards the tent, staring and dropping twigs in her hurry. 'Stella? The Rev's daughter?'

She had always been a nervous woman, Stella thought, surprised. But this alarm over an unexpected visitor was something new.

'That's right.' Stella smiled, trying to reassure her. 'How are you?'

'Why you here?'

'I came to talk. About my dad.'

'But you hated your dad. He told me all about it.'

That threw Stella, and she stared.

Before she could think of a suitable response, Fifi added suspiciously, looking past her towards the vicarage, 'You here on your own?'

'All alone, yes.'

'Well, I don't know nothing about your dad,' Fifi said defensively, adding some of her twigs to the fire pit set a few feet from her tent entrance. 'Them police already come. I told them, it ain't nothing to do with me.'

'I know.'

'So why come see me?'

Stella exhaled slowly, realising this would be more difficult than she had thought. She moved nearer Fifi's fire, which was smoking thickly now. Some of the twigs must have been greener than they looked.

'You knew my dad quite well. I suppose I just wanted to talk to someone about him, someone who would understand.' Stella hesitated. 'May I sit down? Maybe have a drink with you?'

Fifi shrugged. 'Help yourself.'

There were two ripped and discoloured deckchairs beside the fire, one of them heaped with thin plastic bags bulging with old clothes and other prized possessions, dark clothing hung over the back as though to dry.

Stella lowered herself gingerly into the empty deckchair, and smiled encouragingly at her host.

'That's better. Thank you.'

Fifi grunted. She set a small camping kettle on a tripod over the fire, and then tossed the plastic bags backwards into her tent, clearing the second deckchair for herself.

'I don't have no milk. Black coffee do you?'

'I prefer it black.'

Stella watched her shake cheap dried coffee from a plastic bag into two tin camping cups. The last thing she wanted was to drink out of Fifi's famously dirt-encrusted cups. But right now the police only seemed to have one suspect, and it was her. She badly needed to find out who murdered her father, and something told her that Fifi might have some answers. The woman lived here full-time, largely unobserved, right beside the vicarage, in a perfect position to see any comings and goings.

Small wonder the police had questioned Fifi. Taken photographs of her tent. Perhaps even suspected her, as they suspected Stella too.

'So, the police came to see you.' She looked across the smoothly running river to the spring meadow on the other side, lush with small bright flowers among the grasses. 'They must have told you what happened to my dad. How he was found.'

'Don't want to talk about that.'

Stella frowned. 'My dad let you stay here. He was good to you.'

'Not him. Not always.'

She sat forward, perplexed by the sudden hostility in the other woman's voice. 'What do you mean by that?'

'Don't matter now, do it?'

'Fifi, please. Tell me.'

'He touched me.'

The kettle came to a boil and Fifi busied herself making the coffee, stirring the pungent-smelling result with a plastic spoon while Stella stared at her in horrified silence.

'He ... touched you? Oh my God.'

'Just the one time. I didn't like it, and I told him so. He never done it again after that.' Fifi made a face, not looking at her. 'But I never forgot.'

'I had no idea. Did you tell the police?'

'Not then. Bishop knew. He said it were a mistake.' Fifi handed her a tin cup and she took it shakily, some of the scalding black liquid spilling onto her hand. 'But I told the police about it when they come round to ask about the Rev. Seems they already knew.'

She felt utterly lost. Her father had assaulted Fifi?

'I'm so sorry.'

'Why? Weren't none of your fault.'

'All the same … ' Stella cursed her father silently. What the hell kind of man had he been? 'Look, what else did they ask you about? The police.'

Fifi sat down heavily in her deckchair, clutching her tin cup. 'Them police … They wanted to know where I were that day. Sunday. And after. Like they think I done it.'

'You too, huh?'

'I told them, weren't me.'

'Of course not. You're not like that. You're not a killer.'

Though now she knew that her dad had upset Fifi badly. Sexually assaulted her. And God knows what else.

One time, she'd said. But was she telling the truth?

Could Fifi have revenged herself on the vicar with wandering hands by murdering him? Or perhaps killed him accidentally. He might have come down here, maybe late at night, and tried it on again …

Fifi stared gloomily into her tin mug. 'Don't ask, don't tell. That's what your dad always said.'

The sound of mowing from the churchyard had stopped. Stella could hear birdsong from the meadow, and the gurgling rush of the river. It was easy to see why someone would want to live down here in a tent, free from bills and the trappings of domestic existence. Less easy to

'Why did he say that, Fifi?' When she didn't respond, Stella watched the other woman intently. 'Is there something else you're not telling me?' There was a long silence. 'Do you know something about how my dad died?'

Fifi looked up at last, her face scared. 'Me? No.'

'Are you sure?'

After gulping down a mouthful of hot coffee, Fifi suddenly leant forward and whispered, 'Like as not they'd slaughter me if I was to say, and no mistake.'

Stella was shocked. 'Who would slaughter you?'

'Not a word, they said,' Fifi told her, her tone conspiratorial. 'I'm to keep my bloody mouth shut or else. So I'm keeping it shut, see? Coz they can do what they like to me. Worse than your dad. And there won't be no questions asked and no police coming, neither. Not for the likes of me.'

'*They*? Who are *they*, Fifi?'

But Fifi merely shook her head, staring at the ground, her mouth shut.

'Come on now, this is me,' Stella said persuasively. 'You know me. You can trust me. Give me a name, at least.'

'No, no, no!'

Abruptly, Fifi jumped to her feet, spilling her coffee everywhere. Her old jacket was soaked with its dark stain. But the gesture seemed somehow staged, as though for the benefit of someone watching their conversation. Like a way of demonstrating her lack of cooperation.

'You … You better go now,' she said hoarsely, waving a hand towards the vicarage. 'Get out of here. I don't want to talk no more.'

'But – '

'You ain't the police. I don't need to talk to you.'

'I'm sorry, I didn't mean to – '

But Fifi had stopped listening, her face closed and obstinate. She threw herself down inside her tent and zipped up the entrance flap. Like pulling up a drawbridge. Through the thin material, her face pressed against it darkly, she shouted, 'Get lost!'

'Fifi, for God's sake – '

'I got nothing to say to you. Nor to them police neither.'

And that was that.

Stella waited a few minutes, but there was no more noise from the tent. In the end, she got up and bent to leave her cup beside her fire.

'Thank you for the coffee and the chat,' she said to the air. 'I'm really sorry if I upset you. I didn't mean to.'

One of the various items of clothing draped over the back of Fifi's deckchair was a thick black hoody with some kind of silver wording across its back. Only a few letters were visible. Two large shimmering O's.

She paused, frowning.

It wasn't the usual tatty and outsized second-hand clothing Fifi tended to wear, mostly leftovers from church jumble sales, the kind of unwanted items that never sold. This hoody looked almost new, and definitely expensive, not jumble sale material.

Tweaking a fold of the soft, thick material, she uncovered the full words in silver with a sense of disbelief.

On the back of the hoody was COLD MOON COVEN, below a crescent symbol like the astrological sigil for the Moon.

Cold Moon Coven.

They'd slaughter me …

What the hell had Fifi got herself involved with?

CHAPTER FIFTEEN

'Sorry for the interruption, sarge, but I think you need to see this.' Ronny placed a black Hewlett Packard laptop on Jack's desk and made a few rapid keystrokes.

'And what is *this,* exactly?' Jack asked, frowning.

'Penhaligon's laptop.'

Jack lowered the document he'd been reading. 'Which Penhaligon?'

'The Reverend.'

'I thought his laptop was missing?'

'So did I.' Ronny went to lower the blinds on the office window behind them. It was almost noon, bright spring sunlight dazzling off the angled computer screen. 'We found this yesterday in the church vestry when we went back for another search. In a locked cabinet. That church warden guy – '

'Peter Harbut.'

'That's the one. Seems he found his 'lost' spare key to the church, after all.'

'Convenient.'

'Well, he let us in for a good look around the church. Which is when we turned this up.' Ronny tapped the black laptop. 'Luckily, it didn't take long to get past the security on it.'

'Okay, so what have you found? Anything interesting?'

'Nothing incriminating in the documents. Looks like the Rev was pretty good at keeping a clean profile. But there was this one thing … '

'Go on.'

'Our dead vicar had just created a YouTube channel, set to private. Views by invitation only. One short film uploaded about a fortnight ago.' Ronny opened a browser window and clicked a link. A film thumbnail appeared, clearly visible now in the darkened office. 'We found this link to it in an email Penhaligon sent out a couple of days before he died.'

Jack sat up. 'Who did he send it to?'

'Round-robin to about five people. No names, just nicknames and numbers. We've got someone chasing them up with the service providers.'

'Good work, constable. Let's see this film, then.'

'Sarge.'

Ronny clicked the Play symbol, and it started.

The film had been taken with a handheld camera, shaky and amateurish, somewhere dark and wooded. A procession through trees, with flaming torches and chanting. Very *Wicker Man*, Jack thought, leaning forward to get some sense of location, but without any luck.

Robed and hooded figures came into focus, their faces hidden in deep shadow as they swayed through the woods, chanting.

'Any ideas where this is?'

'Could be Pethporro Woods, by the look of it. But somewhere deep in. Right off the official pathways. I've got someone chasing that up too.'

'Excellent.' Jack watched the brown-robed figures with distaste. 'Now tell me we can identify these crazies and I'll be a happy man.'

'Only one definite ID.' The constable pointed to the screen as the procession came to a halt in a clearing. The lead figure threw back his hood and raised his arms in a gesture of invocation. 'The Reverend Penhaligon.'

'Jesus Christ.'

'But this one ... ' Ronny paused the film and indicated the shorter, more rounded figure to Penhaligon's left, whose hood was pushed back a little, revealing the curling ends of long dark hair. 'This one looks like a woman, sarge.'

'Stella Penhaligon?'

'Could be.'

Jack drummed his fingers on the table, studying the grainy image on the film. He knew there was a chance the vicar's daughter was closely involved in all this. But he didn't like the idea.

Ronny hit play again.

The robed figure's sleeve slipped as she raised her torch higher, displaying a coloured tattoo on the inside of her right wrist.

Jack tapped the screen. 'A tattoo.'

'I didn't see that before. Does Stella Penhaligon have a tattoo like that?' Ronny paused the film again and they both studied the design.

'Not sure,' Jack said at last. 'I think she's been wearing long sleeves whenever we've met.'

'We could bring her in again. Take a look for ourselves.'

'On what grounds, though?' Jack shook his head. 'Her lawyer would make mincemeat of us. Besides, all this film proves is that one Penhaligon was into some weird shit, and that one of these freaks wandering about in the woods with him is a woman with a tattoo on her wrist. It doesn't mean that woman killed Penhaligon.' He leant back, staring gloomily at the robed figure on the screen. 'But I bet she knows who did.'

Ronny frowned. 'Could that be Fifi Maggs, do you think?'

Fifi Maggs. The wild-looking homeless woman who lived in a tent near St. Joshua's. They'd gone down to her campsite by the river to ask her a few questions, mostly about any visitors to the vicarage. But she'd claimed not to have seen a damn thing.

Plus, they'd been told Fifi Maggs had made a complaint against the vicar not too long ago. Sexual assault. Only it had been blown off by the church, apparently. She'd refused point-blank to talk about that with them. But it would make a strong motive for murder.

Jack pictured the woman by the river for a moment, then shook his head again wearily. 'Nice idea, but the hair's wrong. And she's stockier than this woman. Taller, too.'

Brilliant. More pieces to this puzzle that didn't fit.

'Well, if you fancy a trip out, sarge, I have an idea how to find the owner of that tattoo.' Ronny closed the laptop. 'And if it turns out to be Stella Penhaligon, I say we bring her in for another round of questions, lawyer bullshit or not.'

The tattoo parlour in Pethporro was down a narrow side street, with a gun store on one side and a New Age bookshop on the other. Ronny stopped outside, peering through the window. 'See there, sarge?' He pointed to a display of tattoo designs in the window. 'That's the one on our chanting woman's wrist. A red rosebud with a serpent round it. One of their special in-house designs.'

'How on earth did you recognise it?'

'My sister-in-law's got one on her ankle.'

Jack glanced at him, eyebrows raised. 'The sister-in-law with the Corgis or the sister-in-law who got married in a black dress?'

'I think you can probably guess.'

They went inside, both grinning. The bell over the door jangled noisily. There was nobody in sight. A slow day in the tattoo business, Jack thought, studying the photographs of designs and satisfied customers on the walls.

'Hey there.' A smiling blonde in denim shorts and a green midriff top sauntered through the bead curtain at the back of the parlour, both legs covered with tattoos, her belly decorated with a coiled snake. 'How can I help you guys?'

'And you are?' Jack held up his ID.

She frowned at his card, then sighed. 'I'm Tasha. What's he done now?'

'*He*?'

'My boyfriend, Sam. He runs this place with me, though he's away at a festival all this week. I presume you're here about him?'

'That depends.' Ronny showed her a copy of the wrist tattoo from the film, the design blown up on the photocopy, with only the edge of a brown sleeve showing. 'This is one of yours, isn't it?'

She nodded. 'Sam's own design. You want one?' She looked Jack up and down speculatively. 'I can do you a good discount. Since you're police.'

'We need a list of everyone who's had one of these.'

'Are you kidding?'

'It looks quite new. So maybe in the past two years, for starters.' Ronny frowned. 'You do keep a record of each transaction, don't you?'

'Sure we do, yeah.' Reluctantly, Tasha pulled out a ledger from under the counter and flipped it open. 'But we don't always take a full name. Sometimes people pay cash and only give a first name. Or a nickname.' She bit her lip. 'Or no name at all.'

'We'll take our chances.'

'Look, do you have any idea how many of those little rose-serpent tattoos we've done? Literally bloody hundreds.'

'Shouldn't be too hard. We only need *wrist* tattoos.'

Tasha rubbed a hand around the back of her neck, looking unimpressed. 'Okay, I'll take a look in the book, see if any sales match that description. But I can't guarantee a result. Sam doesn't keep these records as well as me. So whoever got that tattoo might not have been put down in the book.' She nodded to the plastic seating along the side wall. 'Better make yourselves comfortable, officers. This could take a while.'

CHAPTER SIXTEEN

'You look awful,' Julie said, and sat down beside Stella on the sofa. 'I'm so sorry this has happened to you. I know that you and your dad didn't get on so well. It wasn't an easy relationship, from what you've said in the past. But this ... The way he died ... ' She put an arm about Stella's shoulders and gave her a tight hug. 'And then the police all but accusing you of having something to do with it?' She shook her head. 'They must be mad.'

'Or desperate,' Claire said, handing Stella a bowl of crisps as though hoping to cheer her up with some fattening food. 'With no real leads to go on. That's what they say on the TV, isn't it? The police have no leads to go on?'

Nick steered Claire into the kitchen. 'Why don't you put the kettle on, Claire? I expect Stella's gagging for a cup of tea.'

'Oh, of course.' Claire disappeared.

Nick came back to perch on the edge of the sofa in their small living room. 'How are you, Stella?' He studied her face with a look of genuine concern. 'I'm so sorry I couldn't wait for you the other night. I wanted to hang on and drive you home. But the police made me leave. Practically frogmarched me out of there, after giving me their version of the Spanish Inquisition.'

'It's okay, the whole thing took ages anyway.'

Stella smiled up at her friends, trying to appear cheerful. Or as cheerful as it was possible to be after your father has been chopped into pieces and you've been accused of doing it, she thought grimly.

She'd been sitting cross-legged in the quiet house for several hours, searching online for anything to do with witches and covens in their area. Especially for the Cold Moon Coven. But with almost no success. Apart from a few veiled references on a Magickal Forum to a moon-worshipping coven in North Cornwall, she's found nothing useful.

Julie glanced at her laptop, still sitting open before her. 'What have you been doing? Astrology?'

'Research, actually.' Quickly, she explained about her visit to Fifi Maggs and the black hoody she'd seen there. 'Only there's no mention of a Cold Moon Coven anywhere. Not in Cornwall, anyway.'

'What is a cold moon?' Claire asked, having been eavesdropping while the kettle was boiling. She carried through a pot of tea on a tray with some mugs. 'It doesn't sound very romantic.'

'It refers to a Full Moon that falls in December. Hence 'Cold,' I suppose.' Stella referred to her notes. 'Some people call it the 'Cold Moon rising over the mountains,' or even a 'Long Nights' or 'Yule' Moon. Basically, the last full moon before Christmas.'

'But it's spring.'

Stella smiled at Claire. 'The coven must have decided to take that name for some reason. Perhaps because it was first formed around then. Or one of the coven elders has a birthday in December.'

'What are coven elders?'

Nick shot Claire an irritated look. 'Stella's had a difficult time lately. Maybe not so many questions all at once would be helpful.'

'Sorry.'

'No, it's okay. I want to talk about this.' Stella closed her laptop. 'A coven elder is just someone who's been in the coven longest, or is actually the eldest one there. It usually refers to a founding member of the coven.' She grimaced. 'I've been on my own all afternoon, with this awful stuff going round and round inside my head. It's good to get it out in the open. Also, maybe one of you might be able to help.'

'How?' Julie patted her hand.

'Well, on that forum I found … The comments were about two years old, but there was someone asking about covens in North Cornwall. A hedge witch of some kind.'

'A hedge witch?' Nick made a face. 'What in God's name … ?'

'It's what they call a witch who practises magic alone. Not in a coven.' Stella checked her notebook again. 'Anyway, this hedge witch was tired of working alone, and wanted to join a coven. One of the other forum members said there were no covens near Pethporro, and that if she wanted to attend one in her immediate area rather than travel, she'd have to start one herself.'

'Start a coven? Here in Pethporro?'

'I know.' Stella sighed. 'Anyway, there was no way to find out who everyone was on that forum. They all had generic magical names. But one of them mentioned that there used to be a coven who met at Penway Garage, back in the eighties, and she could try tracking down the members of that coven for starters.'

Julie blinked. 'Penway Garage?'

'I searched online, but I couldn't find anything.'

'That's not surprising,' Julie told her with a frown. 'I remember that place. Penway Garage. It was out by Pethporro Woods. Only it closed down in the mid-eighties, after they built the bypass. No more heavy traffic going that way, I suppose, so not as much need for fuel.'

'Seriously?' Stella stared at her, astonished.

'There's a plant nursery there now. I think it's called … Beverley's Blooms.'

'I know where that is,' Nick said quickly.

'Oh my God.' Stella flung her notebook down, grinning. 'I've been sitting here for hours, totally stuck, and now … This is incredible. Thank you so much.' She rubbed her tired eyes, glad not to be staring at a screen any longer. 'I feel like I'm finally getting somewhere. '

Smiling, Claire handed her a steaming mug. 'That's what we're here for. To unstick you. And make tea.'

But Julie was still frowning. 'How is that helpful though, Stella? Why are you so interested in this coven?'

'The way Fifi reacted when I was talking to her … There was just something suspicious about it. In all the time I knew her, I don't remember Fifi being interested in the occult. Then suddenly she has this brand-new hoody that belongs to a coven?'

'Maybe it was donated to her,' Nick said, 'or she found it somewhere.'

'That's possible, I suppose.' Stella wasn't convinced. 'Though after what I saw at the vicarage, all that pagan stuff my dad had hidden away, I think there has to be a connection between him and this coven.'

Julie nodded warily. 'But shouldn't you go to the police with this information? You're … You're not considering going after the coven yourself, surely?'

They all looked at her expectantly.

Stella cupped her hot mug, wondering how best to answer that. 'The police already think I killed my father,' she said simply. 'Or that I'm involved with whoever did. If I go to them about this, and it's nothing, it'll look like I'm deliberately wasting police time. Or trying to mislead them.'

'And if it *is* something?' Nick asked, looking worried. 'If someone in this spooky coven really is connected to your dad's murder?'

'Then I go to the police.'

'When, exactly?'

Stella shrugged. 'As soon as I've seen this coven in action. Maybe if I see the members of the coven, I'll recognise someone. Someone who might have had it in for my father. Though I have no idea who or why. I just have this strong instinct about it …'

'Your bloody instincts again,' Nick muttered.

'I was right last time.'

He shrugged but did not deny it.

'It's Beltane in a few days,' Julie said quietly. 'First of May. The pagan fire rites that mark the start of summer.'

Nick stared at her. 'And you know this how?'

'I dabbled in the occult when I was in my twenties.' Julie hesitated. 'Before I got into teaching, obviously.'

'Oh, obviously.'

Claire must have seen his expression, because she bit her lip as though to keep from laughing. 'Better be careful, Nick,' she told her cousin glibly. 'She could turn you into a toad.'

'This is serious,' Julie snapped, and her girlfriend sighed, looking away.

'You think this coven will be out to celebrate Beltane on the first?' Stella asked, watching her.

Julie stood up and went to the window. She looked out at the early evening sky, her back turned to them.

'It does seem likely, yes. It's one of the biggest pagan festivals of the year. Though you shouldn't go alone. Not out to Pethporro Woods. Those woods aren't safe at night at the best of times.' She looked round at Stella, her face sombre. 'But especially not when you're spying on a secret ritual.'

CHAPTER SEVENTEEN

Jack got out of the car and stood waiting for Ronny to lock it. The house was set back from the road, a ramshackle place, the yard littered with old engine parts and rusting, broken-down cars, several of the upstairs windows boarded up, and some scraggy-looking hens pecking in a desultory fashion at seed scattered on a patch of grass out front.

'Paradise Cottage,' Ronny read off the cracked sign on the gate. 'This is definitely it. Doesn't look much like paradise.'

'Maybe it did once.'

'I wonder if she's in.' Ronny walked to the front door and pressed the bell several times. There was no sound from within, nor any response. 'I think the bell's broken.'

'Try knocking.'

Ronny had taken a step back and was peering up at the top windows. 'Sarge?'

'With your knuckles? I believe it's what people used to do before the advent of technology.'

Ronny threw him a withering look, then knocked.

After about thirty seconds, the door was flung open and a young, dark-haired woman in hipster jeans stared out at them. Her black T-shirt had COLD MOON COVEN emblazoned across it in silver letters. She had silver rings on almost every finger, and a small crystal pendant on a silver chain about her neck. She had a hard face, blunt and unapproachable. Jack reckoned she had to be about twenty-five, maybe older. Though with her hair up in a ponytail and no make-up on, like today, she could probably pass at a glance for a teenager.

She had a small but distinct pot-belly, and had unbuttoned the top of her jeans to accommodate it.

Pregnant, he thought.

'Who are you two, then?' She studied Ronny, obviously dismissing him, then looked Jack up and down more thoroughly. 'What do you want?'

'Miss Jasmine Carr?' Ronny asked.

'Who wants to know?'

'I'm Detective Constable Myles and this is Detective Sergeant Church. We'd like a word with you, please. Shouldn't take long.'

'Yeah? What about?' She was scowling now, and had glanced nervously over their shoulders more than once.

'Expecting someone else?' Ronny also looked back at the woodland road, which was empty and silent. Apart from the odd tractor, there wasn't much traffic this far from the main road.

'Sorry to disturb you.' Jack stepped forward, trying to keep things civil. 'May we come in, Miss Carr?'

'Do I have any bloody choice?'

'We do need to speak to you quite urgently. Better here than at the station, I would have thought.'

Her scowl turned even uglier. 'Whatever.'

Ronny was already in the hall, looking around. The constable knocked a cardboard box with his boot and a black cat leapt out, hissing. It glared at them both malevolently, ears flattened to its skull, then dashed past them into the yard.

The place was a mess inside as well as out, Jack thought. But he smiled at the woman. She wasn't exactly welcoming. But she also didn't look like someone who could decapitate a man in his sixties before chopping his body into pieces.

It was possible she wasn't alone here though. Or was expecting someone to arrive who might present more trouble than she did.

'Do you mind if I sit down?' Jack asked politely.

He wandered into the cluttered kitchen and found a pine chair that didn't have either cat hairs or rubbish on it, and sat without waiting for her response. There was a dog barking somewhere nearby. Possibly a neighbour's, though he hadn't seen any other buildings nearby.

He nodded to Ronny, who grimaced and got out his notebook and pen.

'We just need to ask you a few questions, Miss Carr,' Jack said, and crossed his legs while she settled against the ancient Rayburn, her arms folded defensively across her chest, half-hiding the words COLD MOON COVEN on her T-shirt. 'If that's okay.'

Cold Moon Coven.

The name of the coven they'd seen prancing about in robes on the YouTube video, perhaps?

'Whatever.' Her pouting face exuded sullen dislike. 'Go on then, ask your stupid bloody questions.'

'We're interested in your tattoo,' he said.

She was thrown by that.

'My … My tattoo? Which one?'

'The little rose and serpent you had done at the parlour in Pethporro.' Jack nodded at her right arm. 'On your wrist there.'

She unfolded her arms and turned her wrist over to reveal the tattoo. Her face was blank with surprise now. 'So I had a tatt done. So what?' She straightened. 'It weren't my first and it won't be my last. It's not illegal to have a tattoo, you know. I'm over eighteen.'

'I can see that.'

'So what do you want? Because if that's all, you can – '

'Tattoos are very useful for identifying people, Miss Carr.' Jack studied her long dark hair, swept up in a ponytail. It had been worn down in the film on Penhaligon's private YouTube link, and of course they had never seen the face. But he felt sure this was the same woman. 'I've seen a film that features you. You and that little tattoo there.'

Her eyes widened on his face. 'What film?'

'Taken in the woods hereabouts, I'd say. You in robes, carrying a lit torch. Hooded. But with that tattoo on show for all the world to see.'

'What?' She was frightened now, her voice hoarse. 'I … I don't know what you're talking about.'

'Would you like to see it?' He held up his phone, as though about to show her the film. 'Just in case you've forgotten you were there.'

She shook her head, staring from him to Ronny, and then at the wall clock. She looked frantic. The woman was definitely expecting someone to arrive, and it was obvious she didn't want them in the house when that happened. Which was interesting, to say the least.

'Bastards!' she snapped. 'What do you filth want?'

'Have you heard of the Reverend Penhaligon?' Jack saw how her face paled at that name, and pressed on. 'He was vicar at St. Joshua's, over towards Pethporro.'

'I don't go to church.'

He nodded to the crystal around her neck. 'More of a pagan, are you?'

'There's no law against that.'

'Maybe not, but there's a law against murder.'

'Murder? What do you mean?'

'Didn't you know? Haven't you seen the news?'

'I don't have a telly. Can't afford the licence.' She glanced at the clock again. 'Who's dead, then? Who are you talking about?'

'The Reverend Penhaligon.'

Jack watched her face, but although she flinched, she didn't look entirely surprised. More scared than anything else.

'About ten days ago,' he continued, 'probably after Sunday mass, somebody cut the vicar's head off, sliced up his body and buried it in various holes in the ground, and then wrapped his guts around a tree like a red ribbon.' Now he'd surprised her. That was something she hadn't known about. He made sure to hold her horrified gaze while his words sank in. 'A pretty unpleasant sight. His daughter was the one who found him. Or rather, what was left of him.' Jack waited, but she said nothing. 'So, Miss Carr, are you going to help us out? Or shall I just arrest you?'

'Arrest me?' She stared at him, wide-eyed. 'What for?'

'Conspiracy to commit murder.'

'No, no.' She was shaking her head violently. 'I didn't murder nobody. This is bullshit. This is police harassment.'

'But you know something about his death.'

'Of course I don't!'

He looked at her thoughtfully. 'How about *ex luna scientia*?' he said. 'Heard of that?'

'I don't speak French.'

'It's Latin. It means 'Knowledge from the moon.' He pointed to her T-shirt. 'You're part of the Cold Moon Coven, Miss Carr, aren't you?'

'So what if I am? There ain't no law against that either.'

'The vicar was a member too, wasn't he?'

'I don't know nothing about that.' But she looked wildly at the door, then back at him, a sudden flush in her cheeks.

'Miss Carr … '

'No.' She began to tremble visibly. 'I … I can't. I just can't.' She bit her lip. 'You don't understand.'

'Try me.'

'They'd kill me,' she whispered, her eyes tormented.

'Is someone putting pressure on you to keep quiet? Someone else in the coven?' Jack stood up, sure now that he had her, that there was indeed a link to the murderer here. 'Who, Miss Carr? You need to tell me.'

But she said nothing more, wringing her hands, her rings flashing. One of them looked chunkier than the others.

'Is that an engagement ring?' he asked. 'Who are you engaged to?'

She swallowed hard. 'I ... I can't,' she repeated, shaking her head. Her hand went to her belly, suddenly protective. 'He'd be so angry with me. Don't you see that? So bloody angry, he might do anything.' She picked up a plastic basket of washing on the table, as though planning to take it outside to be pegged up. 'And I've got the baby to think of now.'

'And I need a name.'

She shook her head again, remaining stubbornly silent.

How the hell were they going to get any information out of this woman, short of arresting her? And if they brought her into the station, they would only have to let her go again soon enough, given how slim their evidence was. But it would do him no good to lose his temper.

'Just a name, Miss Carr,' he said, trying to coax her into cooperating. 'Then we'll leave you alone, I promise.'

Behind him, Ronny said, 'Steve Watterson.'

Jack turned.

His constable was holding up an envelope with a name and address printed on it. Some kind of bill. Highlighted in red too. A final warning.

Steve Watterson. The name rang a vague bell.

But why?

'Well done,' Jack said, putting the thought aside for now, and looked back at her. 'Is Steve Watterson your boyfriend, Miss Carr?'

Her eyes were wide, tormented. 'That letter's none of yours, put it down,' she spat at Ronny, then suddenly threw the basket of washing at Jack, who failed to duck in time.

Jasmine Carr grabbed up a mobile phone from the kitchen table, slipped through the gap between the table and the wall, threw open a back door into the garden, and was gone before either of them had realised what she was planning.

'Get after her!' Jack told Ronny as he tried to recover his balance, wrong-footed and covered in damp clothing. 'For God's sake …'

Ronny plunged through the back door after her. Suddenly, the barking dog was there, snapping and snarling at him.

'Shit,' Ronny swore, kicking the dog away as best he could, keeping his arms up high. 'Bloody animal!'

Jack ran past the dog, looking for the woman. But it was no good.

'She's gone, sarge.' Ronny sounded furious. 'Over the wall at the bottom of the garden. Probably into the woods. We'll never catch her.'

'Copy that.' Jack was already on his phone. 'Hello? DS Church here. We need to pull in a Steve Watterson of Paradise Cottage, on the west side of Pethporro Woods. And get me whatever you can on any known associates. Friends, neighbours, work colleagues. By the end of today, if possible.' He hesitated. 'And be careful. He could be dangerous.'

They, she had said. *They'd kill me.*

Multiple suspects, then. But exactly how many were there?

He had it now though.

Steve Watterson.

Peter Harbut, the churchwarden, had mentioned something about losing to a local man during the races on St. Joshua's Sports Day. A landscape gardener, he'd said, with obvious distaste, though he'd claimed to 'barely' know the man.

Jack was pretty sure the name had been Steve Watterson.

CHAPTER EIGHTEEN

Stella parked near the western entrance to Pethporro Woods and turned off the engine. There were several other vehicles already parked, half-hidden in the shadows; one was a grey van with *Watterson & Son Landscape Gardeners* printed on the side. A local firm; she recognised the name at once. When the churchyard had needed extending about nine or ten years ago, George Watterson had taken on the contract. She remembered a taciturn, thick-set man with old-fashioned side burns and a grey beard. He had seemed friendly enough, always nodding and smiling whenever she passed.

Mr Watterson had to be over sixty by now, and surely retired. Had his son taken over the landscape gardening business?

She had a vague memory of his son, Steve. He used to go jogging along the coast road when he was younger, risking being mown down by breakneck Cornish drivers. A well-built, brooding sort of man who rarely smiled.

Either way, what was their work van doing all the way out here at Pethporro Woods, past eleven o'clock at night?

She buttoned up her jacket, peering about at the dark woods.

'Now what?' She glanced at Julie in the passenger seat, and then looked around at Claire and Nick in the back. 'These woods go on for miles. Where do we start searching?'

'Follow the smell of burning?' Nick suggested. 'There's usually a bonfire involved in this Beltane Festival, isn't there?'

'Of course.' Julie settled her woollen hat more firmly on her head. 'It's the fire festival. There has to be a bonfire.'

They got out of the car, and began to walk into the woods. The moon was high in the sky, but its light was filtered by the trees.

Julie and Nick had brought a torch each, so kept the track ahead of them illuminated, Nick occasionally flicking his torch beam through dark, close-set trees. An owl hooted mournfully in the distance. Other than that, and the rustle of small creatures in the undergrowth, Stella could hear nothing.

'Perhaps this isn't where they gather,' she said, aware of being glad that her friends had all come with her. Being alone in a dark spooky wood at this time of night would not have been her favourite thing. In fact, on her own she would probably have turned around and got back into her car by now. Or not driven here at all. 'Maybe we got here too early. Or too late. It's after eleven. They could have done their Beltane rites and headed off to the pub for last orders by now.'

Julie shushed her, very much in schoolteacher mode. 'What's that?'

'I don't hear a thing.'

Julie stopped walking. 'No, I mean, what's that smell?'

Claire, beside her, put her nose up to the air, sniffing. 'Burning.' She said looked round at her cousin. 'Follow the smell, did you say, Nick? Well, there it is. Where's it coming from?'

'Over there.' Nick pointed through the trees.

'We have to leave the path?' Julie asked, peering into the dark wood. 'Are you sure it's that way?'

'Look.'

They all followed the line of his arm, and sure enough, Stella could see a flickering glint through the dark trunks. A bonfire, she thought. Which had to mean a clearing of some sort lay that way, because nobody in their right mind would start a fire under the tree canopy.

'Come on,' Nick said, and took Stella's arm. 'Let's go and find these coven types.'

'Witches,' she corrected him. 'Or Wiccans.'

'Can a witch be a man or a woman?'

'I think only a woman can be a witch. But Wiccan is kind of gender neutral, as I understand it. Though men can be warlocks.'

'Warlock.' Nick frowned, cracking twigs underfoot as they made their way through the dark wood towards the growing light of the bonfire. 'That's an odd word. Like Goldilocks. Only you have war hair.'

'I don't think that's how it works.'

'Pity.'

She extricated herself carefully from his arm to go round a tree. 'Can you hear that?' She frowned, glancing round at Julie and Claire, who were walking together a few feet behind them. 'Sounds like … chanting.'

Julie nodded. 'We're close.'

'Torches off now, I think.' Nick turned off his torch and pocketed it, and Julie did the same.

They continued to walk in silence for a while, following the glow in the darkness. The sound of chanting grew louder, as did the crackle of the bonfire, its light clearly visible now. It was a low fire, set in a clearing ahead, just as she had expected, and now she could see dark-robed figures standing in a rough kind of circle about the flames.

'Stella?' Claire grabbed at her sleeve as they came to a halt, still hidden among the trees, about a few hundreds from the chanting figures. 'What now, do you think?' She sounded nervous. 'I mean, are we here just to watch and see who they are and what they do, or are you planning something a bit more … dramatic?'

'I don't know,' Stella admitted. 'I honestly hadn't thought beyond seeing if there was a coven, and if they have some connection to my dad's death. Though how I'm supposed to work that out, I don't know.'

Julie was hanging back.

'You want to go back to the car?' Stella asked her quietly, and held out the keys. 'I'm sorry, I shouldn't have dragged you along tonight.'

'You didn't drag any of us along,' Julie whispered, and hugged her coat close. 'Least of all me. We came willingly.'

'That's right,' Claire agreed, stamping her feet softly to keep warm. 'We could never have let you come here alone, anyway.'

Stella gave Julie a quick hug though. 'You look upset.'

'No, I just ... A case of bad memories, that's all.' On the drive over, Julie had described how she'd got involved with a New Age group when younger, soon after her divorce, and had fallen for the coven leader, a charismatic man who'd treated her quite badly. Later, she had decided she'd had enough of men and had met Claire soon afterwards. No doubt the sights and sounds of this Beltane rite had got under her skin. 'Don't worry about me.'

The chanting had stopped. Now they could hear calls and shouts, and even rhythmic clapping. Something was happening.

But that wasn't the only thing that had changed.

'Where's Nick?' Stella stared around in the darkness. 'Nick?'

Claire frowned. 'He was right here a minute ago,' she whispered.

But her cousin had disappeared.

'There.' Julie pointed through the trees to a shadowy figure crouched near the edge of the clearing, clearly outlined against the dancing flames of the bonfire.

'What's he doing?' Julie asked, sounding puzzled.

'Taking photos,' Claire whispered, 'I think.'

'Oh my God.' Stella could not take her eyes off him, horrified at the danger he was putting himself in. 'If they see him … '

Though it seemed the coven was too busy with the rite they were performing to notice that they were being observed, each member now taking a turn at jumping over a flaming log set in the middle of the clearing while the others clapped and shouted invocations that Stella didn't understand.

'I'm taking Julie back to the car,' Claire said abruptly.

It was obvious she wasn't comfortable with the situation, or with her partner's reaction to the Beltane celebration. And Stella couldn't blame her. She would probably feel just as protective in her situation.

'Here.' Stella handed Claire the car keys. 'I'll find Nick and join you in about ten to fifteen minutes, if you can hang on for us that long?' She felt unhappy leaving her friends on their own in the car park, but equally she didn't want to have come out tonight for nothing. 'I wouldn't mind getting a closer look at these witches too.'

Once the others had headed safely back to the car, Stella crept slowly towards Nick's position, slinking from lichened trunk to trunk, keeping as low as possible. She doubted any of the coven would hear her over the clapping and shouts, but if she got too close, she would probably be visible to the coven members on the opposite side of the circle. And she had no idea how these people might react to being spied on.

They'd slaughter me.

That was what Fifi had said.

An odd word to use.

Not kill, but *slaughter*. Like she was an animal, not a human. Or that's how these people would treat her if she crossed them.

The robed figures had finished their wild leaping through the flames, and were now swaying in a circle, chanting again, heads bowed. Their hoods were drawn forward over their faces, nothing but deep shadow visible this far away. She stared hard at each coven member in turn, but could scarcely tell males from females, let alone recognise any of them.

She recalled the horary chart she'd cast. Lord Ten, her father's significator, had been Mars, falling in the Eleventh House of friends and groups.

Were these the 'friends' that chart had indicated?

Sinking down below a thorn bush at Nick's side, she touched him lightly on the shoulder, then whispered, 'The others have gone back to the car.'

He nodded, lowering his camera.

'We should probably go too,' Stella continued, worried someone might see the glint of his camera lens, and turned to leave.

'Wait.' Nick gripped her coat sleeve. 'Do you know any of them?'

She shook her head.

'You're sure?'

'Pretty much. They're all wearing hoods. Now, let's go.'

At that moment, one of the coven members threw back his hood and shouted, 'Spies! Intruders!'

It was a large, burly-looking man under the shapeless robe. His bald head shone in the firelight, sweating. He pointed at Stella and Nick, and all heads swung in their direction, several of the coven already moving their way with grim purpose.

'Time to go,' Nick said hurriedly.

Stella saw the burly man advancing and suddenly recognised him. It was the man she'd seen in the churchyard the other day, mowing the grass between gravestones. And another man had followed in his wake, his muscular gait somehow familiar.

'Of course,' she hissed, squeezing Nick's arm. 'The Wattersons.'

'Sorry?'

'The van we saw in the car park,' she said urgently. 'Landscape Gardening. Steve and George Watterson. They've have known my dad for years. They're paid to do the churchyard maintenance.' She felt like she was going mad, everything she had known for years suddenly unfamiliar. 'They're part of the coven!'

Another hood fell back and Stella caught a glimpse of Fifi Maggs, bleary-eyed and open-mouthed, crying out some kind of curse as she too charged towards their hiding-place. The homeless woman looked as though she was on drugs, her movements clumsy and uncoordinated, a lack of awareness in her face.

Nick found her hand. 'Quick!'

Stella ran through the dark with him, but it was hard to see where she was going after looking into the flames, her eyes dazzled. Twice, she nearly collided with a tree trunk, and would have stumbled over fallen branches and uneven ground if it hadn't been for Nick at her side.

Her head was reeling. But some things finally made sense. George Watterson must have been within earshot when she was talking to Fifi beside the river. No wonder she had been so frightened. Fifi must have been told to keep quiet about the coven and its activities. But what on earth was the connection between the coven and her dad's murder?

The Wattersons were an old family, well-respected within Pethporro. Had her father found out about the coven and threatened to expose them to the parish?

Belonging to a coven was hardly a high crime these days, though. Why kill a man simply for that? And so horribly too. It made no sense.

Behind them, she could hear the roar of the robed man, ordering the others to follow them. 'Find them! Don't let them get away!' George Watterson's voice was deep and Cornish, familiar and yet alien at the same time. 'They must be punished. This, I command in the name of Hecate and Osiris.'

Punished?

And *in the name of Hecate and Osiris*?

Stella definitely didn't like the sound of that. Hecate was a dark figure, the goddess of magic and witchcraft, while Osiris was the Egyptian god of the dead. Probably not a good thing when they were being invoked against you, she thought.

They kept going, crashing through the woods without caring how much noise they were making, but Stella was no longer sure they were going in the right direction.

'How far to the car?' Stella gasped.

'A couple more minutes?'

'I can't keep up this pace.'

'Me neither.'

She slowed, staring about wildly. 'Nick, I ... I think we're lost. We should have hit the track by now. Which way is it?'

'Shit.' Nick grabbed her arm. 'Come on,' he said in her ear, and dragged her aside into a thicket, with thorns that tore at her clothes and skin. 'Sorry. But you're right. We can't outrun them.' He crouched down with her, both of them trying not to pant too loudly in case it gave their position away. 'We can hide, though.'

A sudden thought struck her. 'But what about Julie and Claire? They'll be sitting ducks in that car park.'

Nick fumbled with his phone and punched out a quick text, then hit Send. 'I've told Claire to get out of here and take Julie home. No point us all getting caught.' Slipping the phone back into his pocket, he grinned at her. 'Well, this is a fun way to spend an evening.'

'Are you crazy?'

He shrugged. 'It makes a change from escorting old gentlemen to the toilet.'

'I wish I'd never suggested this. It's been a disaster.'

'Hush.' Nick held up his hand, frowning. 'Listen.'

Suddenly, the wood was strangely silent. Stella listened hard, but couldn't hear a thing, though she could smell acrid smoke from the bonfire on her and Nick's clothes.

Had their pursuers given up?

Then the sound of engines suddenly filled the woods. Loud, high-pitched bike engines. Motorbikes, she thought, feeling dazed.

'What the hell?' she whispered.

'Christ.' Nick had risen slightly and was peering out through the thicket opening. 'They're on motorbikes.'

'I don't understand. What are they doing on bikes?'

'Hunting us,' he said grimly.

Stella stared at him, horrified, as the reality of their situation sunk in. 'Oh my God,' she said, scared for the first time. 'And we've sent Julie and Claire home. We've got no way out of here.'

CHAPTER NINETEEN

'Okay, you won't believe this, sarge,' Ronny said, dropping a document several sheets thick on his desk. 'The preliminary report from the pathologist's office makes interesting reading. Should be in your inbox by now.'

Jack lowered the book on serial killers he'd been speed-reading while he drank his coffee. It was depressing stuff, anyway.

'Give me a summary.'

It was late at night, gone eleven o'clock. Both of them should have been back at their respective homes by now, with their feet up.

Instead, they'd been out most of the evening on various wild goose hunts, chasing down Steve Watterson from pub to snooker club, and never finding him at any of his apparent haunts. Though Jack still held out hope of running their chief suspect to ground. It seemed unlikely he'd have fled the county, even if his girlfriend had warned him the police were on his tail.

'The vicar's body parts were cut up with a small axe. Though the pathologist reckons some of them have been … ' Ronny paused, making a face. 'Well, I guess "tidied up" is the best description. With what she thinks might have been secateurs.'

'Secateurs?' Jack stared at him.

'Exactly.' Ronny perched on the edge of his desk, one leg swinging. 'Matches our man Watterson, don't you think? A small axe and a pair of secateurs. Definitely the kind of tools a landscape gardener might be expected to have lying about.'

'It certainly makes him more of a likely suspect. Any news yet?'

'Nothing yet, sarge.'

'What about his dad, Watterson senior?'

'His name's George. Nobody at his house though. Maybe the two of them are out together somewhere.' Ronny looked at him curiously. 'You think both Wattersons are involved?'

'She said, *they*.'

'True, but – '

'It would be easier to cut up and dispose of a body with more than one man on hand. Though not impossible to do it alone.' Jack shrugged. 'I'm reserving judgement on the old guy.'

'Sick, that's what it was. God, those intestines … You reckon a father and son could do something like that together?'

'Maybe the father was only helping in order to protect his son. I've heard of stranger things.' Jack frowned at him. 'And get off my desk, DC Myles. You're not in the sixth form.'

'Sorry, sarge.' Ronny stood up, looking awkward.

'How about the Wattersons' work van?'

'No sightings yet. But the details have gone out. As soon as one of our patrols claps eyes on that van, they'll call it in.'

Jack's mobile rang. He glanced down at the screen.

It was his sister.

'Hang on, I need to take this.' He got up and left the large open office, only answering the call in the corridor outside. 'Bernadine?'

'Jack, it's good to hear your voice.'

His sister sounded uncertain. But then, they had barely spoken since his wife's funeral. No doubt she still feared he blamed her for Chloe's death. And maybe he did at some level. But not with his logical mind.

'I'm sorry to call so late,' she added hurriedly.

'It's okay. I'm still at work.'

'Oh.' Bernadine sounded relieved. 'Well, I wanted to check how you were doing.'

'I'm fine,' he said, a little tersely, wondering what all this was about. His sister wasn't one for social calls. Especially this late in the evening. 'Is everything okay with Mum?'

He felt guilty; their mother was in a home, suffering with dementia, but on the outskirts of North London, nearer Bernadine than him. So his sister tended to visit her regularly, where he only managed to see Mum once or twice a year. Not that she remembered him when he did visit.

'Mum's doing well, no need to worry. Still pottering about with her little stuffed dog, yelling at the other inmates. She had a chesty cough a few weeks back, but it's cleared up now. That isn't why I called.'

Jack frowned, waiting for her to explain. But she stayed silent. 'Bernie, if it's not Mum, then what's the matter?' He tried not to sound impatient, though he was anxious to get back to the Watterson situation; he had a nagging suspicion there was something they'd missed about the case. 'You sound upset.'

'I'm sorry,' his sister repeated, her words almost too faint to hear. 'It's the date, that's all.'

'What?'

'Today's date. It would have been … '

'Chloe's birthday,' Jack finished abruptly, and closed his eyes as the awful truth hit him. It was the first day of May. If she had lived, today would have been his wife's fortieth birthday. And he had forgotten the significance of the date. 'Of course.'

'I shouldn't have rung.'

'Nonsense, I'm glad you did. We don't talk as much as we should. Besides, there's something I've been meaning to say … ' He opened his eyes and stared blankly at the station noticeboard opposite. Reminders of important dates and procedures. A charity fund-raiser coming up. 'I blamed you for what happened with Chloe. I shouldn't have done. It was grossly unfair of me.'

'Forget it.'

'What Chloe did … Nobody could have stopped it. She was intent on her own destruction. Ever since the miscarriage.'

'All the same, I ought to have kept a closer eye on her. I knew ... I knew how vulnerable she was.'

She insisted, 'Chloe would have found a way sooner or later. I realise that now. It wasn't your fault, Bernie. I've been wanting to tell you that for a long time.'

There was a short silence.

'Perhaps I could come down to visit you this summer,' Bernadine said tentatively, 'if that's convenient. I'd like to visit Cornwall, see where you're working now.'

'Sure, that would be brilliant. Decide on a date and I'll organise some leave, show you around. Cornwall's great in the summer, especially if you're outdoorsy.' He realised with a pang that he no longer knew what kind of things his sister liked to do in her free time. 'Do you surf?'

'Me?' Bernadine seemed to find that question amusing. 'Only on the net. I'm a Londoner through and through. Institutionalised.'

'A few surfing lessons at Widemouth Bay and you'll soon be converted to the Cornish way of life, trust me.'

They talked about nothing in particular for another few minutes, just catching up. As he was about to hang up, Ronny appeared in the doorway to the office.

'Sarge?' Ronny looked animated, his earlier weariness gone. 'Sorry to interrupt. But we've had a patrol call in a sighting of Wattersons' work van. Out by Pethporro Woods. And they say they can hear motorbikes somewhere in the wood.'

Jack felt an answering leap of excitement. At last!

'Look, I have to go, Bernie,' he told his sister quickly. 'But thanks for the call. I really appreciate it.'

And he did.

Knowing that his sister didn't think he was to blame for his wife's breakdown ... That made a great deal to him.

All the same, Jack knew that when he finally got home from work, he'd be cracking open a bottle of whisky and sitting down to analyse exactly why and how he had forgotten his late wife's birthday. Overwork might sound like the perfect excuse for forgetting such an important date. But he knew there had to be more to it than that.

'*De nada.*' Bernadine sounded relieved rather than annoyed. 'I'll text you a likely date for me to come down this summer.'

'Can't wait.'

Jack rang off and turned to his constable. 'Pethporro Woods, did you say? Not far from Jasmine Carr's cottage, then?'

'Exactly what I was thinking, sarge.'

'So, let's get out there.' He hurried through to grab his coat from the back of his chair. 'And what was that about motorbikes?'

'Dunno, sarge. Could be kids messing about. Though they said there were quite a few other cars parked there. All empty, nobody in sight.'

'At this time of night?'

Ronny shrugged. 'Some kind of meeting in the woods?'

'Jesus … '

Jack remembered the skull and jewelled dagger they'd found in the vicar's secret study, and the YouTube video of the pagan worshippers in hooded robes. That ceremony had been held in the woods too.

'You're thinking black magic shit? That coven again?'

'Sounds crazy, but it's becoming a real possibility.' He recalled the Latin inscription he'd seen on the Reverend's study wall. *'Ex luna scientia.'*

'Sorry, sarge?'

'*Knowledge from the moon.* Something I saw at the vicarage. Okay, tell the patrol to sit tight for now, we'll be there as soon as we can.' Jack snatched up his car keys. 'And if anyone comes back to the car park, they need to prevent them from leaving. Arrest them, if necessary. One of them could be Penhaligon's killer.' He had a feeling something very bad was happening. 'I think we'll need back-up too. Dogs, helicopters, the works. Whatever this is, it stops tonight.'

CHAPTER TWENTY

Stella had somehow lost Nick in the chaos. They had been running side by side, that was what she remembered, aware of pursuit close behind.

Then a motorbike had come roaring across the narrow space between trunks, loud and hot in the darkness, and almost knocked into her. Briefly, she had seen the bearded face of the biker, grinning madly. The younger Watterson, enjoying the chase. She had thrown herself sideways, and banged her head against a stone of some kind, jutting out of the tangle of undergrowth.

Everything had gone black temporarily, and when her head stopped spinning and she was able to move without nausea, Stella found she was alone.

'Nick?' she whispered, but there was no reply.

She wanted to search for him in the undergrowth, fearful he had been hurt more badly. But she was still being hunted. And not only by bikers. There were people on foot too, shouting incoherently, crunching over leaves and twigs. She could hear them getting closer and knew she couldn't stay where she was.

The robed figures from the coven, she suspected, and they were determined not to let her get away. She had seen their secret ritual. Intruded on their cult meeting. Almost certainly gross misdemeanours in their rule book, she thought.

What would the coven do if they caught her?

She couldn't be sure of anything right now. Especially not their motives. But it didn't take much imagination to come up with a few possibilities, none of them very comforting.

Stella remembered Fifi Maggs, the woman's terrified expression as she claimed, 'They'd slaughter me,' and in her mind's eye saw again the bloodless, butchered head of her own father, testimony to the utter ruthlessness of his killer. Or killers.

Perhaps they were all in it together. The thought was terrifying.

Primal fear drove her back to her feet. A trickle of blood was running down her face, she could taste it in the corner of her mouth. She groaned but did not stop, staggering from tree to tree, desperate to get away from them. But how? And which way would get her out of this bloody wood?

Lost, she lurched on in the direction she thought Nick might have been leading her when they got separated, her head aching.

A woman fled past, moaning. Her hood had fallen back.

It was Fifi Maggs.

Stella followed, but slowly, keeping her distance. She didn't think Fifi was dangerous. But she wasn't taking that chance. Minutes later, she thought she was almost safe, seeing lights through the trees. Perhaps she had found the car park at last.

'Shit.'

She ducked behind a tree, grimacing.

That was a torch beam she could see, not car headlights as she'd thought. Someone was searching the woods ahead of them, shining a powerful light over every bush and tree. A member of the coven? Or one of her friends?

Whoever it was, they were nearly upon her.

Stella crouched, trying to make herself as small as possible, and fought a wave of nausea. How bad was her head wound? She probably needed to get to a hospital, perhaps even stitches.

But staying alive had to be her priority right now.

Behind her, in the thicker part of the woods, she could hear her other pursuers getting closer. More shouting, more whooping, and in the distance, the sound of a motorbike being revved as though before a race. With a stab of fear, she understood how the fox must feel as the hounds close in. Perhaps if she were to make a run for it …

The torch beam swept over her position, and she froze. 'Who's there?' It was a man's voice. 'Come out where I can see you. This is the police,'

She recognised the voice, relief flooding her.

'It's me, Stella Penhaligon,' she said shakily, moving out from behind the tree into the path of the bright beam. 'Is that you, DS Church?'

'Stella Penhaligon?' He sounded stunned. 'What are you doing here?'

'It's a long story.'

'I don't have time for long stories,' he said shortly, shining the light right in her face so that she turned her head away, dazzled. 'But you are definitely in the wrong place at the wrong time. Once again.' She could hear suspicion in his voice, and a distinctly unfriendly note. 'You'd better walk towards me, Stella. Slowly now, hands where I can see them ... '

Wincing, she obeyed, lowering her eyes so she didn't have to face the bright torch, the pain in her head acute now.

'My friend's somewhere in the woods still,' she said hurriedly, worried she might pass out before she could get the information out. She was dizzy now, stumbling over the uneven ground. 'His name's Nick. I ... I think he may be hurt.'

Behind her, the roar of motorbikes grew loud again, and now she could see distant headlights flickering through the woods. That madman on the bike coming round for another pass, perhaps. Only this time he wasn't alone.

DS Church was putting a phone to his ear as she reached him. 'Is that blood on your face?'

'I got knocked down by one of those bikes. We'd better hurry ... They're probably coming back.'

'Who are *they*?'

'I only know the Wattersons ... They run a Landscape Gardening business. I forget the younger guy's name.'

'Steve,' he said flatly. 'Steve Watterson.' He spoke into the phone. 'Yes, DS Church here. Where are those dogs? And my back-up? And we're going to need ambulances, at least two.' He listened for a moment, then hung up, putting the phone away. 'Right, let's get you back to the car park, Stella. You can wait in my car until the paramedics arrive. That head wound looks nasty.'

'Wait, there was a coven meeting tonight,' she said urgently. 'The Wattersons are part of it. Maybe the leaders, I'm not sure. I know this probably sounds crazy, but ... the coven may have something to do with my dad's murder.'

'It does sound crazy. But that doesn't mean you're wrong.'

She stared at him. 'You believe me?'

'This way, and no trying to run off, you hear me?' DS Church turned the torch beam onto the woodland floor so they could see their path ahead. 'Okay, look, let's say I do believe you. What in God's name are you doing out here in the woods at this time of night, mixed up with that lot?

'I had to see the coven with my own eyes. Anyway, last time I came to you with a hunch, you weren't exactly supportive.'

'That was about astrology. This is ... evidence.'

'I don't have any evidence.'

'You don't need it. You're not a police officer. What you need is to stay home and leave this kind of thing to the professionals.'

'Whatever.' She staggered against him.

He caught her. 'Christ!'

'Sorry.' Her head was spinning. 'Okay, this was stupid. But it seemed like a ... a good idea at the time.' She half-turned, the roar of bikes in her ears. 'They're coming back!'

CHAPTER TWENTY-ONE

'Get behind me.'

DS Church swung to face the oncoming motorbikes. He flicked the torch across the ground, then stooped briefly, straightening with a thick branch in hand, the wood sprouting with leaves, his torch beam bouncing everywhere as he spun the sturdy branch sideways.

Stella stumbled backwards into a tree trunk, seeing him silhouetted against oncoming headlights set to dazzle.

'Look out!'

The noise of the bike engines were deafening. She thought the detective would be mown down. Then he spun the branch again, jumping swiftly out of the way as one bike skidded sideways, and the other reared up, thick tree branch stuck in its wheel, its rider falling backwards.

Someone pulled her backwards out of the path of the skidding path. 'I've got you,' a voice said in her ear.

It was Nick.

She turned, breathless. 'Oh my God, Nick, you're okay. I thought … '

'Sorry, I looked but couldn't find you in the dark.'

'Me neither.'

Several police officers pushed past them, one grabbing a fallen biker and pinning his arms behind his back. It was Steve, George Watterson's son, his face flushed as he struggled against the police, swearing profusely in his thick Cornish accent.

'Did you kill my father?' she demanded, trying to get near him.

Nick grabbed her arm. 'Stella, leave it to the police.'

But instinct leapt inside her. Stella remembered Fifi Maggs, the palpable fear in her face that day down by the river.

She might not be a detective, but she was used to reading people as she looked at their charts, seeing which planets were more dominant in their lives, and her gut told her these were the men who would have slaughtered Fifi if she'd talked about their secret rituals.

No wonder the woman had run from the clearing as soon as the coven broke up in chaos. Fifi was probably afraid the others would turn on her next, thinking she'd betrayed them.

'I know you did it,' she shouted at the two men, wrenching her arm free. 'But why kill him? Because he was a vicar? And why cut him up like that? Are you sick?'

Old George Watterson struggled up off his motorbike, the front wheel still spinning. She heard him bellowing threats and abuse at DS Church, who was reading him his rights.

'You killed him, didn't you?' Stella screamed, and flinched when old Mr Watterson finally turned to glare at her, bald head gleaming in the torch light.

'Yes, we killed him. But not without good cause.'

Stella clasped her hands to her cheeks. 'I knew it,' she whispered, shocked that her instincts had been so right. 'But … But why?'

'Your father knew what he was risking,' George Watterson snarled.

'What does that mean?'

'Them's the rules,' he spat out.

DS Church had raised his torch beam and was studying George Watterson, his eyes narrowed. 'Rules? What rules?'

'Coven rules.'

'Don't say another word, Dad!' his son yelled, being wrestled to his feet now, several police officers holding him still.

'Oh, what does it matter now? They got us, don't they? It's over.' His father wiped the back of his hand across his sweating forehead, and glanced up as a police helicopter flew over the woods, the trees moving restlessly in its wake, its searchlight pinpointing them on the ground. 'Vicar took what wasn't his to take. He had to be punished.'

'Dad, keep your bloody mouth shut!'

His father ignored him, looking at Stella. 'Your father transgressed. He had to die the death of a transgressor. He chose his own fate.'

'What?' She stared, horrified.

'Dad, for fuck's sake!' his son was shouting.

'Ronny, get Steve Watterson out of here,' DS Church said sharply, and the son was dragged away, still yelling at his father to be quiet.

He nodded at the older man. 'I've read you your rights, Mr Watterson. You don't have to say anything.' He paused. 'But you admit it? You killed Penhaligon?'

'Vicar deserved it. He should have known better. He was one of the founders of our coven.'

'The Cold Moon Coven?' Stella interrupted.

'That's right.' George Watterson looked round at her, almost sneering. 'Yes, vicar ran the church, but he were Wiccan too, through and through. He followed the old ways. So don't go shedding tears for that one.' He nodded. 'Your dad knew what he was doing when he transgressed, just as he knew the punishment.'

DS Church frowned. 'Transgressed? What do you mean?'

'Life, limbs, entrails, face,' George Watterson chanted, a fanatical look on his face. 'Stone and wood his resting place.'

'Sorry?'

'That's how a traitor dies, one who breaks coven rules. And I'm proud of what I done. Vicar had it coming, and no mistake.'

Unwillingly, Stella recalled how she had found her father's remains in the depths of St. Nectan's Glen, half-buried under a beech tree, his entrails wrapped about its lichened trunk. *Wood.* And his decapitated head had been found in the ruins of Tintagel Castle, the police had said, balanced on the ancient battlements, staring out to sea. *Stone.*

DS Church shone the torch across the man's sweaty face. 'You said, he took what wasn't his to take. What did he take, Watterson?'

'My son's woman.'

The detective seemed stunned. 'Jasmine Carr?'

'My son can't father a child. He tried for years with his first wife. Then with Jasmine.' Watterson spat on the ground. 'Only the vicar took a shine to her, didn't he? Started innocent enough. The sex rite at Sabbat, skyclad in the ancient way. What happens on sacred ground don't matter to us.' He shook his head in disgust, his voice thickening. 'But Penhaligon took it out of the circle, started visiting her at the cottage when Steve was out. Then Jasmine told us she was pregnant, and whose child it were.'

Stella felt sick, unable to believe what she was hearing.

Her father had not only been a member of the coven, but had slept with one of the women? And fathered a child with her?

'Was it you who trashed the vicar's study?' DS Church asked him. 'Why do that? What were you looking for?'

George Watterson hesitated, then said reluctantly, 'That weren't me. That were Steve. Bloody fool. He said vicar had a book there, with all our names writ down in it. But we tore that place apart and never found it.'

In the distance, dogs could be heard barking ferociously, and someone shouted, 'Police, don't move!' More members of the coven being discovered hiding in the wood, perhaps. She hoped the police would arrest them all.

How many of the coven had known what the Wattersons were up to?

She was sure Fifi Maggs had known how her father died. Or suspected, at least. Yet she hadn't come forward. Terrified in case the Wattersons came after her next, presumably.

'Ronny, do the honours, would you?' DS Church nodded to his constable, who began to lead the man away.

Stella limped after George Watterson. 'Wait, I don't understand. Couldn't you and Steve have thrown him out of the coven instead?' Her head was throbbing with pain, but she couldn't let it rest. 'It was just a ... an affair. My father shouldn't have slept with her. It was wrong, I know. But you didn't have to kill him, for God's sake.'

'Vicar knew the rules,' Watterson repeated, surly now. 'He broke his vow to the old gods. He defiled my son's woman. And we made sure he paid for it.'

'Keep walking,' the constable said, pushing him forward.

DS Church blocked her path when she would have continued to question him. 'I'm sorry, Stella,' he added in a low voice, blocking her path as she would have followed, 'but I can't allow you to talk to him anymore. Both the Wattersons are under arrest. We need to get them back to the station, get their confessions down. I'm sure you understand.'

Stella groaned. 'But he didn't deserve to die.' She watched Watterson disappear through the trees, her vision blurring with tears. 'And not like that.'

DS Church gave her an apologetic look, and then hurried towards some police officers emerging from the trees with other coven members.

Nick shook his head. 'Stella, the guy's plainly crazy. Both him and his son are bonkers, anyone can see that.

Grown men dressing up in robes and worshipping the Full Moon, or whatever they do … '

'It's not like that.'

'Well, whatever it is, of course your dad didn't deserve to die. But it's time you got that head injury patched up.'

'I'm fine,' she insisted.

'Sure you are. You just look like an extra from a zombie movie. Come on, let's get out of here.' Nick put his arm around her waist, supporting her towards the flashing blue lights. 'I don't know about you, but I could do with a stiff drink. And a few days off work.'

DS Church caught them up in the car park, on his phone again. Finishing his call, he shot her and Nick a wary look.

'Stella, I'm sorry about your father. But you need to leave the investigation to us now, okay? Those coven members weren't messing about. You and your friends could have been badly hurt tonight. Or worse.'

'I know,' Stella agreed, thinking of the transits she'd seen in her own chart before leaving the house. Mars clashing with her natal Uranus, plus a strong eighth house vibe that had been dogging her all month.

She'd known she could be risking her life. But she hadn't felt like she had a choice. Not if she wanted to be sure what happened to her dad.

Nick glanced at DS Church. 'I took a few photos back there, by the way,' he said, clearly pleased with himself. 'Mad coven members leaping through the flames. Will I be okay posting them on social media, do you reckon?'

The detective gave him a dry smile. 'I reckon,' he said, 'you'd better give them to me. And no social media posts. This is a live police investigation.'

Nick grimaced. 'I had a feeling you might say that.'

The car park at Pethporro Woods was awash with flashing blue lights. A dog van stood open, two dogs padding about beside it, being fussed by their handlers. There was an ambulance too, just drawing out onto the main road, and another still waiting, its double doors open, the interior brightly lit. Overhead, the police helicopter was still hovering, though as they left the woods it banked left and began to fly away, its bright searchlight gradually fading above the trees.

Perhaps they had caught everyone now, she thought, watching the helicopter disappear.

'Thank God, the others are okay.' Nick pointed out Julie and Claire, standing by the car talking to a police officer. They both looked cold and very worried.

'Hey,' he called across to them, and Julie turned, smiling in relief.

George Watterson was being put into the back of a police car. There was no sign of his son. She guessed the police must have already whisked him away.

Deeply and immeasurably tired, Stella found herself wishing she could sit down, even if just for a few minutes.

She also wanted to check in with her friends, and apologise for having put them all in so much danger tonight. If she hadn't been so insistent on coming out to see the coven in action herself …

DS Church raised a hand to his constable across the car park, and then hesitated, glancing back at her. 'I'm afraid we'll need a statement from you and your friends as well,' he said, 'and an explanation of what the hell you were all doing here tonight.'

She nodded, too exhausted to care.

'But first, you should probably have that seen by the paramedics,' he said, gesturing to the gash on her head, 'before you collapse.'

'This woman, Jasmine Carr ... Her baby ... Has she had it yet?'

He shook his head silently.

'And did you know all that?' she asked as he turned away. 'About the Wattersons? The coven? What they did to my father?'

DS Church shrugged without answering, and then continued walking.

Stella put a hand to her head, grimacing. She'd had enough of men trying to hide the truth from her. But at least she knew roughly what had happened to her father. And why.

Nick helped her towards the waiting ambulance.

'Thanks,' she told him, and patted his hand on her arm. 'But I'm okay to walk on my own now.'

Her body was trembling, and everything hurt like she'd been run over, but she didn't want his help. She didn't want anyone's help just now.

She could do this herself.

Stella had never been so frightened in her life as when running alone through the woods, pursued by those maniacs on motorbikes. Yet she didn't regret what she'd done. Not one bit. Because if she hadn't come here tonight, angering the coven by spying on them, the police might never have arrested the Wattersons, and she would never have discovered what they'd done to her father.

'Here,' the paramedic said, smiling as he helped her up into the ambulance. 'Been in the wars, haven't you?' He turned to fetch a kit. 'Any double vision? Dizziness? Don't worry, we'll soon get you fixed up.'

Stella smiled automatically, but tonight had been a shock, and she was still reeling from it. She spent her life sitting down in front of an astrological chart, piecing together the truth of a life or an event, everything controlled and methodical, even the worst aspects kept at a safe distance.

But it was the truth about her own father she'd been piecing together this time, and it made her feel sick to know how little she'd known him.

Reverend Charles Penhaligon, vicar of St. Joshua's, Pethporro.

She thought of that fixed star conjunct his Taurus Sun. Caput Algol, the Head of the Demon, a 'blinking' star at 26 degrees of Taurus.

It had been known throughout history as one of the most evil stars in the heavens, associated with violence and misfortune, as well as death by decapitation, according to Ptolemy. She had previously dismissed its reputation as mere superstition. A story to scare the credulous. Unfortunate in some cases, perhaps, but not actually *evil*.

But now she could see where it had been pointing her.

Her father had been a secret coven member for years, a pagan and an occultist, and God knows what else. He had also been sexually involved with some woman she didn't even know, this Jasmine Carr, with whom he'd apparently fathered a child.

An unborn child who would be her half-brother or sister.

Stella did not know how to deal with that revelation. But first, she had to bury what remained of her father. And try to forgive him.

EPILOGUE

Jack poured himself a whisky, drew the empty cardboard box towards him, and looked down at the items on the coffee table. Items he'd been gathering from around the house all day.

It was more than three weeks since the newsworthy arrests out at Pethporro Woods. The majority of the Cold Moon Coven, taken in for questioning in their hooded robes and wellies. To his surprise, Peter Harbut had not been among the coven members. He'd been wrong there. Though most of them had turned out to be ordinary law-abiding citizens, who merely liked to get their jollies from dressing up once a month and chanting in Latin.

But George and Steve Watterson had taken the Wicca thing more seriously, as a search of the father's property had shown, out on the coast road only a few miles from St. Nectan's Glen.

In George's cellar, they'd found a stone altar to a horned devil, covered with candles, bones – not all of them animal – and dark crystals, etc. Plus a laptop full of what appeared to be homemade pagan porn, mostly featuring Jasmine Carr in the nude, dancing about in the woods or enjoying Satanic sex rituals with her boyfriend, and sometimes old George too.

Not a pretty sight, he thought, grimacing at the memory.

But no wonder the two men had become murderous when she admitted to her secret affair with the Reverend Penhaligon, and worse, that she was carrying his child.

There had also been clear DNA links between their premises and the vicar, including his blood, inexpertly cleaned up from the flagstone cellar floor.

The newspapers, both local and national, had had a field day with the story. CORNISH WITCHES BEHEAD VICAR, and so on.

It had been the old guy's idea to kill the promiscuous vicar, according to Steve, though his son had admitted to chopping up his remains and burying them at St. Nectan's Glen, following instructions in some print-on-demand manual of arcane Satanic rituals they'd bought on Amazon.

Not surprisingly, Steve Watterson had been furious at Penhaligon for succeeding where he had failed in fathering a child with his girlfriend Jasmine.

Jealousy.

One of the oldest motives around.

Though Jack suspected there had been political jealousy behind the vicar's gruesome murder too. The Reverend Penhaligon had helped found the Cold Moon Coven, and some of the other members had spoken of frequent bust-ups between the vicar and George Watterson.

It seemed that a death among the coven's leadership would trigger a promotion in the hierarchy, and George had stood to benefit. As it was, he'd been the one leading the ritual that night in the woods. Top man at last, master of all he surveyed. And he had risked everything for it.

He'd heard that Steve and his dad weren't speaking to each other anymore. That Steve would be mounting a separate legal defence. Apparently, he was none too pleased that his father had confessed to being an accomplice to murder without even consulting his son.

Whatever the truth of it, the courts would have to decide now which of the men was the more guilty. Bar the inevitable paperwork, his job was done.

And he'd met an interesting new person along the way.

Stella Penhaligon.

He hoped she was coping. The astrologer had been so distraught over her father's murder. Yet he knew from experience that the immediate aftermath of a loved one's death was not the worst part. Having to carry on with your everyday life afterwards, to pick up the pieces and somehow find a new way of existing without them …

That was the hellish part.

Jack picked up a silver lighter from the table, and turned it over to read the engraving. TO CHLOE, WITH ALL MY LOVE, JACK

He hesitated, then dropped it into the cardboard archive box.

She'd been an on-off smoker. The odd cigarette over drinks after work or at the weekends. Her dad hadn't liked Chloe smoking as a teenager, so she had stubbornly stuck with the habit into adulthood. Jack hadn't much liked her smoking either. But he'd accepted it as part of her lifestyle.

Now she was gone. Gone forever. And it was time he accepted that too.

Jack looked down at the tableful of items he'd gathered from around the small house they'd shared as husband and wife. Old photos, memorabilia, souvenirs of holidays they'd taken together, little knick-knacks, the kind of thing that had meant something personal to her but not him.

He picked up each one, studied it carefully, like saying goodbye all over again, and then dropped it into the archive box.

When the table was empty, he put the lid back on the box, and carried it into the spare room with all her other things. Clothes, coats, shoes, suitcases. The bare mattress stacked with the dresses he'd removed from their wardrobe. Like Chloe herself had laid them all out on the bed only a few minutes ago, unable to choose which one to wear.

Jack stood in the doorway a moment, looking around at all her stuff. His dead wife's things. He didn't know why he couldn't bring himself to get rid of them. It was almost as though he was still always waiting for Chloe to come home. As though he still expected the phone to ring one day, or the doorbell to go, and it would be her on the step, laughing at his astonishment and saying, 'It was all a misunderstanding, Jack. A case of mistaken identity. Some other woman stepped under that train and I … I … '

One day, he would take them to a charity shop. Say goodbye properly. For now though, this was an important first step. He had read about it online. Some bereavement counselling site that Bernadine had recommended. Small steps, that was all it took. This first. Then later …

He turned off the light, shut the door, and went through to the brightly-lit kitchen to make his dinner.

THE TENTH HOUSE MURDERS

Following a spate of gruesome local murders, police are no nearer to finding with a connection between them or a killer

...

DS Church approaches astrologer Stella Penhaligon for help, despite his misgivings.

Other fiction by Jane Holland

GIRL NUMBER ONE (#1 UK Kindle Chart Bestseller)
LOCK THE DOOR
FORGET HER NAME
ALL YOUR SECRETS
LAST BIRD SINGING
MIRANDA (WHY SHE RAN)
THE HIVE
DEAD SIS

UNDER AN EVIL STAR (Stella Penhaligon Thrillers #1)
THE TENTH HOUSE MURDERS (Stella Penhaligon Thrillers #2)
THE PART OF DEATH (Stella Penhaligon Thrillers #3)

Printed in Great Britain
by Amazon